The Bad Wife

Kim Reynolds novels *by* Jacqueline Seewald

The Bad Wife

The Inferno Collection

The Drowning Pool

The Truth Sleuth

The Bad Wife

A Kim Reynolds Mystery

Jacqueline Seewald

PERFECT CRIME BOOKS

THE BAD WIFE: A Kim Reynolds Mystery. Copyright © 2014 by Jacqueline Seewald. All rights reserved. No part of this book may be reproduced, transmitted, or stored by any means without written permission except in the case of brief quotations embodied in critical articles or reviews. For information address Crime@PerfectCrimeBooks.com.

Printed in the United States of America.

Perfect Crime Books™ is a registered Trademark.

This book is a work of fiction. The characters, entities and institutions are products of the Author's imagination and do not refer to actual persons, entities, or institutions.

Library of Congress Cataloging-in-Publication Data
Seewald, Jacqueline
The Bad Wife: A Kim Reynolds Mystery / Jacqueline Seewald
ISBN: 978-1-935797-56-2

First Edition: April 2014

This novel is dedicated to my husband Monte,
who supports me in every way possible.
It is also dedicated to my family and friends.

Acknowledgements

I would like to acknowledge the help provided to me by Andrew Seewald, Esquire, able criminal defense attorney in New Brunswick, New Jersey. Also, a special thanks to all the fellow librarians from around the world who have supported the Kim Reynolds mystery series by purchasing copies for their libraries.

"As to marriage or celibacy, let a man take which course he will, he will be sure to repent."

Socrates

"So heavy is the chain of wedlock that it needs two to carry it, and sometimes three."

Alexandre Dumas, *fils*

"One shouldn't be too inquisitive in life
Either about God's secrets or one's wife."

Geoffrey Chaucer, *The Caterbury Tales*

"They dream in courtship, but in wedlock wake."

Alexander Pope, *The Wife of Bath*

Chapter One

"Must be fate," a masculine voice said.

Kim Reynolds dropped the head of lettuce she'd been examining, and it rolled across the floor.

"Didn't mean to startle you," Mike Gardner said.

She looked up. "I didn't expect to run into you in the produce section of the supermarket." Kim did her best to ignore the attraction she felt for him.

"I'm not stalking you," he said.

"I never thought you were."

He gave her a small smile that implied he didn't believe her. Then he scooped up the head of iceberg lettuce and handed it back to her. "You decapitated it."

"You would think that way," Kim said. She meant to sound stern but ruined it by smiling.

"Hey, I'm a cop. Guess I tend to think in violent metaphors."

Kim looked around. "Mike, don't you usually take the girls shopping with you?"

"Evie stayed late to try out for a school play. She's into drama now. I dropped Jean at a friend's house so they could study together—at least I think that's what they're doing." Mike Gardner studied her with a probing look. "So how have you been?"

"You mean since you saved me from being killed?"

He shrugged in a nonchalant manner, but his expression was one of concern. "I wasn't going to mention that. You still teaching at the high school?"

She looked away. His sharp gray eyes saw too much. "I gave my notice."

"How come?"

"One of the reference librarians at the humanities library is going out on sabbatical. I was offered the chance to go back to the university in my old job. It's what I'd rather do."

"Congratulations." She sensed his warmth was genuine.

"Thanks."

"I guess your principal was pissed off?" He searched her face.

Kim shifted uneasily, pushing a lock of dark auburn hair behind her ear. "Hank said he kind of expected it. I guess I disappointed him. I confirmed what he thought all along, that the work was more than I could handle."

"Sweetheart, don't be so hard on yourself. You did a good job with those kids under difficult circumstances. No one could have done better."

She smiled, appreciating his kindness. Mike Gardner had a good heart; no one knew that better than she.

"So are you still seeing Principal Anderson socially?"

Kim stiffened. "No, I'm not. But it's really none of your business."

He drew closer. "I beg to differ. I think it's very much my business. Everything about you concerns me."

Kim breathed in the male scent of him, and she felt a surge of emotion. She kept a tight rein on her feelings most of the time, but it wasn't easy with Mike so close to her.

"And how is your wife?" she said in as even a tone as she could manage.

Mike had the decency to look down at the floor. He clenched his hands, shoved them into his jeans pockets.

"Evelyn is still living with you, isn't she?"

"She's living in the house. We're not living together. I think you know that."

"Do I? Nothing's really changed, has it?" Her voice sounded hollow, which was the way she felt.

Mike's face hardened. "I can't just kick Evelyn out. She's got no place to go. No job, no prospects." He sounded defensive.

Kim watched him. She was a little psychic sometimes, and the talent had helped her solve murders. But she'd gotten no warning, psychic or otherwise, about the woman she had believed was Mike's ex-wife. Evelyn Gardner had never filed the paperwork for the divorce decree. Evelyn had made that clear to both Kim and Mike when she returned. Long ago, Mike had filled out the necessary forms and mailed them to Evelyn. As he explained it to Kim, he thought the marriage legally ended.

"You've offered Evelyn money to sign the divorce papers and get out of your life, haven't you?"

"I have," Mike acknowledged.

"Why won't she accept?"

Mike lifted a hand and ran it through his dark hair. The touch of gray at each temple made him look older than his thirty-nine years. "I don't know. She says she wants to reconcile with me, but I don't believe her. Evelyn's up to something. I'm just not sure what it is."

"I guess she doesn't shop, cook or clean?"

"Got that right," Mike said, his expression sheepish.

Kim shook her head. "You're tough with criminals. Yet you let her get away with murder."

"I know. Bert says I ought to kick her sorry butt out the door."

Kim agreed with Bert. Mike's sometime partner and fellow homicide investigator was a good judge of character. Bert St. Croix was a strong woman both emotionally and physically who did not tolerate bad behavior in others. Mike normally didn't suffer fools either. He had a good amount of common sense and an uncommon insight into people. She knew his nickname around headquarters was The Psychologist. Homicide investigations were usually handed to him for that reason. But apparently common sense was not so common when it came to dealing with his wife. Now why was that?

"Mike, do you still have feelings for Evelyn?"

He met her level gaze. "I don't love her, not anymore. She left the kids and me, went off with another guy. She was the one who claimed she wanted a divorce. It all happened a long time ago. We hadn't seen her for years. I put her out of my mind until she showed up a few months ago. You know that. I never would have asked you to marry me if I thought Evelyn and I weren't divorced."

"You could still love her though. Emotions don't need to make sense," Kim said. "Feelings aren't always logical."

"True. But the girl I fell in love with back in high school doesn't exist anymore. People change. Evelyn isn't the same person and neither am I."

Kim bit her lower lip, lost in thought. "Maybe you only thought you knew her. Some people are very clever about disguising their true nature when it suits them or they see some benefit."

He took her hands. "The plain truth is I love you, Kim. You and I, we belong together. If I'd met you first, I never would have married Evelyn. But she is the mother of my two daughters. For that reason alone, I feel I owe her something." Mike's expression was earnest. Kim knew he spoke with honesty and integrity. That was in part why she loved him.

Kim Reynolds understood family obligations. Didn't she have her own after all? She said, "I respect and admire your sense of duty. You're a good, decent man. And I have strong feelings for you too. But I can't allow us to become involved again under these circumstances. It wouldn't be right." Kim removed her hands from his, swallowing hard.

Mike gave her a curt nod and exhaled a deep sigh. "Yeah, I kind of knew you were going to say that. You've got a strict code of ethics."

Kim glanced around to make certain that no one was listening in on their conversation. "I have reasons for feeling this way. There are things you don't know about me."

Mike raised his eyebrows. "Secrets?"

Kim shrugged. "I wouldn't call it keeping secrets."

Mike gave her a questioning look. "I guess this isn't the time or place to talk about personal matters."

"No, it's not," she agreed.

"I admire you for taking the moral high road, but selfishly speaking, I regret that we aren't together the way we should be." He squeezed her hand. "We are going to find a way to make it work. Don't give up on me. Don't give up on us."

Kim found herself unable to speak, too choked with emotion. She offered a quick nod.

"I'll tell the girls I saw you."

"You do that," she managed to say. "Give them my love. Of course, I don't think Evie's forgiven me for walking out of your lives."

"She understands," Mike said.

"Does she?" Now it was Kim's turn for a probing look. Mike's teenage daughter had been hurt and angry the last time they spoke.

"She can be a hothead," Mike said. "Evie told me how she blew up at you. She's sorry about it. Told me she realizes how kind you've been to her, like a big sister."

"I'll visit with the girls one day when Evelyn's not around, if that's all right with you."

Mike gave her a big smile. "That would be great. They both miss you."

"Even Jean? Now that her mother's back?"

"Even Jean. The novelty's worn off. She's beginning to realize Evelyn never was much of a mother to her and never will be. As for little Evie, she can't wait for her mother to leave again permanently. We all miss you in our lives."

Kim found herself choking back a sob, which was crazy because she never cried, never became emotional. She was saved from embarrassment when a stock boy rolled a cart of apples by her.

The youth turned around and stared with a look of surprise.

"Miss Reynolds, I didn't expect to see you here."

"Hi, Gary, we all have to eat, even teachers."

As the boy from one of her English classes moved on, Kim felt some of the tension leave her. They were in a public place and it was time to finish selecting produce, not have an emotionally charged conversation with an ex-lover. She let out the breath she'd been holding.

Mike must have felt the same. He gave her a relaxed almost lopsided smile that she found endearing. "I've got a mystery for you to solve."

"You're the detective, not me," she said.

"I wouldn't say that. You solve my cases when I can't."

"Mike, I'm a reluctant sleuth at best."

"And a reluctant psychic?"

"You know it."

"Well, here's an easy mystery to solve. Why do supermarket prices keep increasing while product sizes continue to shrink?"

"Inflation. I don't need any special powers to answer that."

"But the government tells us there is no inflation." Mike gave her an innocent smile. "Shouldn't we believe those in authority?"

"That's a rhetorical question."

"Guess it is at that. Okay, ready for some supermarket humor?"

Kim groaned. "You tell the worst jokes."

"Is that why you always laugh at them?"

"I'm polite."

"So I've noticed. It's one of many things I like about you. Here goes."

Kim tilted her head to one side glancing at him from the corner of her eye. But he was undaunted. She realized he was attempting to defuse the tension that had built between them.

"Man walks up to an attractive young woman in a large supermarket and says, 'I lost my wife here in the store. Can you talk to me for a couple of minutes?' Puzzled, the woman asks 'Why should I talk to you? How would that help find your wife?' He answers: 'Because every time I talk to a good-looking woman my wife appears out of nowhere.' Kim, you're frowning. You're supposed to at least smile."

She shook her head. "Sorry, the joke made me think of Evelyn."

Mike let out a deep sigh. "Things are really messed up, aren't they? All because of Evelyn. Okay, I guess there's only one thing left for me to do." Mike partially pulled back his leather bomber jacket revealing the holstered gun clipped to his belt. "Put a period to the problem. I'll have to kill my wife. Shoot her dead. That would settle matters once and for all. Then you and I could finally be together."

At that moment, Kim noticed Gary, red-faced and shaken,

staring at Mike Gardner open-mouthed. He called out to her. "Miss Reynolds, s-should I call the police?"

"Son, I *am* the police," Mike smiled and winked.

Gary didn't see it. He ran in the other direction, knocking over a display of canned beans. Kim hadn't been aware of the boy's return. Her attention had been fixed on Mike. Kim was mortified. Gary had obviously eavesdropped on part of their conversation and thought she was in danger. Kim shook her head at Mike.

"What? You're giving me the same look you probably reserve for trouble-making students."

"That was irresponsible." She narrowed her eyes. "You frightened poor Gary half to death. And he's not one of the difficult students who might deserve it."

Mike shrugged, his manner unconcerned. "You're not going to continue working at the high school so what difference does it make?"

"Evie might hear about it. You don't want your daughter upset or embarrassed by your behavior, do you?"

"If Evie thought I'd really shoot her mother, she'd applaud."

"That's not funny, Mike," Kim said, placing her hands on her hips.

"Honey, I was only joking." But Kim wasn't certain. "Want me to go after the kid and let him know I wasn't serious?"

Kim shook her head. "I doubt he'd believe you."

Chapter Two

"*Mike, tell me* you didn't do that!"

"What? I was trying to make a point." His look was all innocence.

"Yeah, well the point's on top of your head," said Bert St. Croix. She shook her head, and ebony braids bounced.

Gardner shrugged. "You're as much of a hard ass as Kim."

"Thanks. Think I'll take that as a compliment. And here I thought you were the only guy I know who doesn't have balls for brains. Then you go and prove me wrong. Scaring stock boys in a supermarket. I can't believe you'd be guilty of such juvenile behavior."

"Didn't notice him. I'm in a tough situation. Sometimes it gets to me. Anyway, I was just kidding around, trying to get Kim to lighten up."

"That bitch you married is playing you, man. Throw her out on her skinny ass! Get rid of the user. Stop being a sucker." The color of Bert's *café au lait* face deepened. She pointed a finger at him. "You usually show more sense than most people. You're a mature man. You want to impress Kim. I get that. But you'll have to find a better way to go about it than threatening to kill your wife in front of witnesses."

Gardner frowned. "Okay, I concede I acted like an irresponsible jerk."

"It's not like you. You got me worried. I would hate to see you doing something you'll regret. But you got to know as long as Evelyn's on the scene, Kim's going to keep her distance. She wouldn't be the woman you love if she didn't."

"Guess you're right. At least I'm rid of the competition. She dumped the high school principal."

"I think you ruined that relationship for her, making her think he might be a murderer."

Gardner's eyes met Bert's. "I really thought he was a killer."

"You mean you wanted him to be. Face it, you were jealous."

"Could be," Gardner said, his jaw jutting. "You're pretty hard on me, you know."

"Yeah, we women of color are known to take a tough stand with men we care about. Comes with the territory."

Gardner realized his personal life was a mess. He had acted stupidly and now regretted it. It wasn't typical behavior for him. He prided himself on having plenty of common sense and objectivity. Right now he knew only one thing for certain: he wanted Evelyn gone from his life.

Mike was good cop. He had a keen, intuitive understanding of people—all except for that bitchy wife of his. He had a blind spot when it came to her. It disgusted Bert to see that Evelyn Gardner was getting away with her helpless female act. Mike and Kim were both her friends. She wanted them together and happy. As her mama used to say: *we're all headed for the same destination; what matters is how we get there.*

Someone needed to intervene, to help Mike and Kim find their way back together. Seemed like Evelyn was determined to make life difficult for them. Mike and Kim were miserable being apart. But short of murder, what could she do to help them? The situation was a difficult one. Evelyn Gardner wasn't the type of person you could reason with.

Bert had an uncomfortable feeling that it could all end badly, maybe even tragically. She tried to shake the feeling. She'd already known a lot of sorrow in her twenty-seven years and didn't want to know more if it could be helped. But being a cop, she supposed that went with the job description more than she would like to admit.

Chapter Three

"*So when are you* coming down to Florida to visit us?" Ma asked.

"Soon. I promise. I'm looking forward to it. It seems like everyone around here goes to Florida for vacation during the winter months if they can get time off and can afford it."

"It's lovely down here in the winter. Can you come for the Christmas holiday like we discussed?"

"I had intended to visit during the recess, but I turned in my resignation at the high school. I'll need to get organized. I'm going back to work at the university." Kim waited for her mother to respond. Ma was taking her time, ever thoughtful.

"Will you be happier there?" Ma asked finally. Did she imagine that her mother sounded doubtful?

"I think so. I hope so." Kim hesitated. It was hard to know what would be good for her.

Since Evelyn Gardner had returned and surprised Mike with the announcement that she'd never filed the divorce papers, Kim had felt an emptiness in her life. Her heart hurt, she literally ached inside. No use dwelling on that. It wasn't going to help her situation or solve anything.

"I like doing reference work," she said. "It's a good feeling helping students and professors with their research. Helping people is something I learned from you, Ma."

"Is the realtor having any luck finding a buyer for our house?" Her mother sounded embarrassed. Ma never knew how to handle a compliment.

"No interest in the house so far. The agent says the real estate market is still doing badly, especially for lower-priced homes. Hopefully, the economy will pick up. Speaking of that, have you found work down in Florida?"

"Part-time only, but I intend to locate a fulltime job soon. There are a lot of convenience stores around here."

Kim couldn't remember a time when her mother didn't work. She visualized Ma with her graying hair and warm brown eyes looking weary but loving.

"Will you be able to come down here soon?" Ma persisted.

"I hope so. I'll do my best."

"Maybe you can get away for a week or so? I miss you, Karen."

"I'm Kim now, Ma."

"If you say so, dear. I don't understand why you can't still be Karen Reyner."

Kim sighed. They'd had this conversation before, but her mother stubbornly refused to accept Kim's explanations.

"Ma, I don't want to be known as Carl Reyner's daughter. The man was a monster. He killed those people at the V.A. hospital for no good reason."

"Carl was troubled. He was not a monster. He came back from military service traumatized. If only you could have known him before he went overseas. He was a different person."

Kim tapped her fingers against her telephone with an air of frustration. Ma would never stop making excuses for the man. There was no point putting her mother on the defensive. It always drove a wedge between them.

"I don't want to argue about him. He's dead. He killed himself. It's over and done."

"I suppose we'll just have to agree to disagree," Ma said.

"There is something I would like to know, something we really haven't discussed."

"Oh? What's that, dear?"

Kim shifted on the sofa which also served as her bed in the small studio apartment. "You told me that Carl wasn't my real father."

There was a pause on the other end of the phone. "That's true." Kim heard her mother's tone become guarded.

"I sensed Carl wasn't really my father even when I was a small child. He always made it clear he disliked me."

"That isn't true, dear. In his way, he loved you."

"I didn't misinterpret his behavior toward me, Ma. I never felt we were a family in the true sense of the word. I'd like to know who my real father happens to be."

Now the pause became stone silence.

"Ma, are you still there?"

"Yes, dear, I'm here. The thing is, well, I think I told you we were both married. He was unhappy in his marriage and so was I — but for different reasons. Carl was in and out of the V.A. hospital. He'd been wounded physically and mentally. It turned out Carl wouldn't be able to father a child. I always wanted children. I didn't deliberately set out to have an affair with a married man or to have a child by him. But we were both lonely and unhappy and we comforted each other."

"I understand. I am an adult. I don't condemn what you did and I certainly don't intend to pass judgment. But, Ma, I think I should know who my father is."

Again the silence at the other end. Her mother could have been at the other end of the world. God, it was frustrating!

"Ma?"

"I'm thinking."

"What is there to think about? Don't I have a right to know? For health reasons if for no other."

"I know you, Karen. You're stubborn. You'd want to find him, wouldn't you? You wouldn't let it rest until you did. You'd want to meet him, wouldn't you?"

Kim bit down on her lower lip. "What would be wrong with that?"

"Everything. I never even told him I was pregnant. We parted before it became obvious."

Kim stood up and began pacing, holding the phone to her ear. "I don't understand you."

"It's mutual," her mother said. "Please, let's not discuss it anymore. Can't we just drop the matter?"

"This isn't the end of it," Kim said.

"No dear, I suppose not." Her mother let out a long-suffering sigh. "You have the tenacity of a pit bull."

When the conversation ended, Kim slammed the phone down. She loved her mother but they viewed life differently. Kim knew one thing for certain. She would never knowingly have an affair with a married man, no matter the circumstances. She might love Mike Gardner, but their relationship was over as long as he remained married to Evelyn. Much as Ma loved her, that love didn't make up for growing up without knowing her real father.

Chapter Four

Mike Gardner arrived home with two large bags of groceries. As he placed the produce into the fridge, he thought about Kim, about having run into her at the market that last time, how he'd hoped it would happen again. But it hadn't.

Evelyn sauntered into the kitchen. Funny how beautiful he thought she was back in high school. Now the bleached blond hair and heavy make-up gave Evelyn a hard, cold appearance. She looked jaded, old beyond her years. He had to wonder how he'd ever found Evelyn attractive. He supposed they'd both changed over the years.

"The girls didn't come home with you?"

He was glad to hear Evelyn expressing some interest in their daughters. He said, "They'll be home for dinner."

"Are you cooking or picking something up?"

"Maybe you'd like to fix dinner for a change?" He realized his tone sounded sharp.

She laughed, the sound shrill, grating. "I never liked cooking. I gave up on it a long time ago."

"You gave up a lot of things. Tell me, what do you do all day while I'm at work and the girls are at school?"

Evelyn's eyes narrowed. "That's none of your business."

"I kind of think it is since you're living in my house."

"*Our* house."

"It hasn't been since you moved out all those years ago. You left us without a word. That boyfriend of yours dump you out in L.A.?"

She shrugged. "He turned out to be a loser."

Gardner faced her. While Evie and Jean were out, he reasoned, they could do some straight talking. "You can't stay here much longer. You're going to have to get a job and a place of your own. I want you to sign off on those divorce papers so we can be permanently and legally done."

Evelyn licked her lips. "Why? So you can be with that uptight librarian?"

"Kim is a good, decent person. She cares about other people. She does her best to help them."

Evelyn pursed her lips as if she were sucking on a lemon. "I didn't know you went for the saintly martyr type. But that figures. She won't complain when you put her second to your job. She won't mind the lonely days and nights. She'll worry you might get shot by a killer or drug addict. Yeah, that Mother Teresa clone is just perfect for you. Me, I'm through worrying about any man."

"Knock it off. We both know you worried more about chipping a fingernail than you ever did about me."

Evelyn placed her hands on her ample hips. "There was a time when I cared, but a woman has to put herself first."

"I cared plenty about you," he said, his expression tight.

"Not enough."

Gardner felt the anger rush to his head, his temples throbbing. "So you cheated on me and ran off with some wannabe actor."

She gave him a quick shrug. "We both intended to make it big in Hollywood. Neither one of us did. But I still have hopes."

He confronted her. "I've offered you money to leave here. What else do you want?"

She smiled at him like a cat playing with a mouse. "You didn't offer nearly enough."

"I'm a cop. You know that. I don't earn a fortune."

"True. That's why I've come to a decision. You'll have to sell the house. I want half of what it's worth."

Gardner stared at his wife in disbelief. "I built this house with my own hands."

"Let's not be so dramatic about it. It's a house. You can rent an apartment."

He balled his hands into fists and stuck them into the pockets of his jeans to keep from punching her. "That's what you want for your daughters, to deny them their home?"

She studied her long, blood-red fingernails. "Plastic surgery costs money, lots of money. I need it to compete with younger women for acting roles."

Mike shook his head. "Evelyn, I know you acted back in high school, and you were good, but you're not a kid anymore. Can't you look into doing character roles?"

Her face turned an unpleasant shade of purple. "I'm not going to play old women."

"You're the mother of a teenager."

"I had Evie when I was very young."

"Not that young. Look, this obsession you have with being a big movie star, it isn't healthy. You're about as likely to become a famous actress as you are to win the lottery."

Her features contorted with her rage. "I never should have married you. Never! I wasted too many precious years. I should have had a career when I was young. You need to pay me back for that."

Mike had never felt such anger toward anyone else in his entire life. He couldn't have hated a serial killer with more fervor. His muscles trembled. He wanted to reach for his service revolver and shoot his selfish bitch of a wife over and over again. He would like nothing better than to blow her head off and shut her nasty mouth forever.

Chapter Five

Kim Reynolds was home, or at least it felt like home. She hadn't expected to ever return to the humanities library at the university as a reference librarian. Kim felt terrible about leaving the high school position in the middle of the school year, but there were plenty of unemployed teachers eager for her job. The position had been filled immediately. No one was ever indispensable or irreplaceable—not in this world.

"I shouldn't admit this but I'm glad they hired you back," Rita Mosler said. "I missed you."

"Thanks," Kim said smiling at the older woman.

"Don't go getting misty on me. The fact is, you're the only one who could tolerate calls from that idiot who wants to know the cast of every movie ever filmed," Rita said in a tone that could sour milk.

"As I recall, our movie lover is a lonely old man who just wants an excuse to talk to other human beings."

Rita Mosler turned up her needle nose at this bit of information. "Well, he should join a senior group and stop bothering us. Next time the geezer calls, I'm telling him to phone the public librarians with his stupid questions. We're an academic institution. Honestly, it's ridiculous. They'll tell you anything to get you to hurry up and get them the information they want. Don't let people like that play on your sympathy." Rita was an old-timer and somewhat jaded by the job. Students rarely went to Rita for help if they could avoid it. Rita was razor-tongued. Her caustic manner frightened students almost as much as her bony, arthritic fingers that resembled bent twigs.

Later as if on cue, Rita received a phone call from the Mad Movie Fan, as she referred to him. "Take it for me," she said, thrusting the phone into Kim's hands. "I can't stand to talk to that idiot again. If I do, I'll give him a piece of my mind."

Kim got on the line. It was the old man's shaky voice just as she remembered it. Some things didn't seem to change. She smiled to herself. He asked her to look up information for him and she did so as he held on. He wanted the original cast list, director and producer of *The Maltese Falcon*.

"One of my all-time favorites," she told him.

"Mine too. Thank you, young lady."

"It didn't seem like too much to ask," Kim said after she'd finished with him. "He's likely a shut-in or something. Obviously, he doesn't own a computer."

"He's a pest. Calls everyday with some silly question. I'd like to wring the old geezer's neck."

"The man's just lonely," Kim reiterated. There were times when she would have liked to phone somebody and just talk for no particular reason herself. She understood feelings of isolation only too well.

On her break, Kim walked around the library. She'd only been gone half a year and yet there were changes in progress. She realized how much she'd missed the campus and this library in particular. She had even missed the unique smell of the place.

She studied the modern art on the walls, the swirls of blue and green carpeting. Large plants decorated the front windows. It was an impressive red brick building with five levels holding well over a million volumes.

At this time of day, the computer labs were the busiest part of the library. She passed the undergrad reading room and decided to take a quick walk outside. She stepped beneath the concrete pillared entrance. A brisk wind gusted from the west. The temperature was falling, a reminder that winter was her least favorite season of the year. Since she'd not bothered to pick up her coat, Kim shivered and decided to return to the sanctuary of the library.

A large sign pointed downward proclaiming a "coffee café" on the atrium level. This confused her. The basement level had always held the bound journals. Had they been moved? If so to where?

Kim asked Rita that question when she returned.

Rita shook her head. "No one really knows. My opinion? They've tossed the old periodicals. The library's gone modern and digital."

"But not everything's available online," Kim protested.

"Having a coffee café is considered more important," Rita said. "Best not to question the decisions of those in authority. You remember how that got you in trouble before?" Rita frowned at Kim, pushing back her frizzy, gray hair.

Kim said nothing. Of course Rita was correct. Kim realized she did tend to over-think many things rather than just accept the inevitable. Too often she saw things others did not. It was definitely more of a curse than a benefit.

As if to drive this home to her, a student approached her at the reference desk that afternoon. He was slim and fair-haired and appeared nervous. She pegged him as a freshman.

"Could you tell me where the East Asian art collection is being displayed?"

She smiled hoping to help the young man feel more comfortable. "Certainly, just walk back outside to the main corridor, look to your right and you'll see the sign that says East Asian Studies. The art is on display inside that area." She reached beneath the desk and brought out an orange brochure.

"Are you new at the university?" she asked.

He flushed slightly. "Does it show? I'm a freshman. I still don't know the campus very well. Some of my classes are on the main campus like Expository Writing and others are at different campuses. I'm an art major," the boy explained.

"Well this will provide basic information for our social science and humanities library but not for the art and science libraries on the other campuses," she said.

"Thank you." He flashed a grateful smile.

As the young man reached over to take the printed brochure from Kim, his hand brushed hers. Kim had a sudden reaction. Her head began to spin. She saw the young man as if through a kaleidoscope. He was confronting another boy, taller and darker. They appeared to be in a dorm room standing beside a computer.

The blond boy said, "Kev, you've been spying on me through the Webcam on your laptop. I could kill you for that."

"Let's face it, Dennis, you're a wuss. But you provide good entertainment. Who's that boyfriend of yours anyway? He's got a nice ass."

Dennis punched his roommate in the face. Then everything spun away.

"Miss, are you okay?"

"What?" Kim put her hand to her forehead. She was weak and sick to her stomach.

"You spaced out for a second there. Are you epileptic or something?"

Kim shook her head. "No, I'm fine. Low blood sugar. Guess I forgot to eat enough today."

"Well, take care," the young man said, his brows knitting together.

Kim touched his arm gingerly. "You might consider changing roommates if that's possible."

He stared at her, mouth slightly open. "Why? What do you know?"

"Just a feeling. Call it intuition," she said thinking perhaps she should not have spoken. How could she explain about her visions? She didn't even understand them herself. He'd think she was insane.

The young man started to walk away, then turned back and looked at her one more time as if she had the head of Medusa. God, it was embarrassing! And yet how could she not say something? At least she'd provided a warning. Her vision implied that something terrible would happen between the two roommates. One of them was destined to kill the other. She shuddered.

She'd seen death before. Yet there was no way to prevent it. Often she felt herself to be cursed like the mythological Cassandra.

Kim was still feeling shaken when she arrived back at her apartment that evening. The vision she'd seen was still troubling her. It had succeeded in ruining what should have been a happy day. Could she have done something more to help the young man? As she agonized over that thought, the telephone began ringing. She reached over and picked it up on the second ring, answering with a quick hello.

"Is this Kim Reynolds?"

She answered in the affirmative.

"I want you to come over to my house."

"Who is this?" Kim asked, although afraid she already knew the identity of the speaker.

"Evelyn Gardner. You and I have something in common—my husband."

"Evelyn, you and I have nothing to talk about." She managed to keep her voice calm but firm.

"*Au contraire*. We've got a lot to discuss. My husband hasn't touched me since I came back." Evelyn's voice was sharp with accusation.

Kim kicked off her shoes and sat down on the sofa which doubled as her bed in the small studio apartment. "I don't know what you think, but you're wrong. I've had nothing to do with Mike since you returned."

"He still wants you, though I can't understand why. I'm about ready to blow this lousy place. There's nothing here for me."

Kim almost retorted that her daughters were here and wasn't that reason enough to remain, but then she thought better of it. She didn't want to provoke an argument with this unpleasant woman. It would be pointless.

"You still want Mike too, don't you? Handsome hunk like him? Sure you do. Well, I could sign those divorce papers. Then he'd be able to marry you."

Kim didn't think for a moment that Evelyn was being honest with her. "What would you expect in return?"

Evelyn laughed. It wasn't a pleasant sound. "Come by tomorrow evening around eight pm. I'll make certain everyone else is out so we can talk."

"We can talk right now."

"No, this has to be in person. Don't tell anyone, especially not Mike." With that Evelyn slammed the receiver down.

Kim remembered a statement that Socrates supposedly made: "By all means, marry. If you get a good wife, you'll become happy; if you get a bad one, you'll become a philosopher." She hoped for his sake Mike had a philosophical bent. Kim stood there for several minutes holding the receiver in her hand.

That night, she dreamed of Carl Reyner.

"What's the matter, girl? Do I scare you? Are you afraid of ghosts?" His features were distorted.

"I'm not afraid of you. I know you're dead. Go back to hell where you belong."

"Is that where you think I am?" He laughed. "You don't know a damn thing."

"When I was little, I wanted you to love me. I believed you were my father. But you weren't my father. I know that now. You can't hurt me anymore."

He floated above her, hazy, indistinct. "You're wrong. You didn't respect me when I was alive," he said. "You'll pay for that." Carl's voice was mean, menacing, threatening.

Kim woke up in the dead of night sweat dripping. She turned to look at her clock radio and saw it was only two a.m. Just a bad dream. It meant nothing. The Bible may have viewed dreams as prophecy but she would not. Kim did her best to get back to sleep. But she couldn't shake a sense of wrongness. She realized that Evelyn must have subconsciously reminded her of Carl. She sensed a darkness of the soul they both shared.

Chapter Six

The day was cold. Winter whispered in the air. Kim felt tired all through the day at the library.

She fought the negative feelings that plagued her. It helped that she was kept busy.

In the afternoon, as she replaced ready reference materials under the desk, Kim heard a familiar voice.

"So glad you're back. It's wonderful to see you working here again." Kim looked up into the smiling face of Professor Don Bernard. He was a very attractive man with fair hair and light-blue eyes. Kim knew him to be a favorite with the English majors, the girls in particular.

"It's always a pleasure to help you with your research, Dr. Bernard," Kim said.

One patrician brow rose. "My, we've become awfully formal. I'd like to renew our friendship. Are you dating that police detective?"

"No, I'm not seeing anyone," she admitted, casting her eyes downward.

"I won't be a hypocrite and say I'm sorry."

Kim found herself smiling.

Don Bernard said, "We must do lunch together soon. It's been too long." His voice was deep and seductive. He took her hand in his for just a moment.

Rita joined them at the information desk. Don Bernard straightened his posture. "Ladies, always a pleasure. I'll be back in a few days. I have a new journal article to research."

She and Rita watched him stride out of the reference section.

"That is one sexy man," Rita observed with a sigh.

Kim smiled at her. "I didn't think you noticed."
Rita frowned at her. "I may be old but I'm not dead."

That evening, Kim returned to her apartment after a tiring day at work. Her head hurt. Kim took down her hair and brushed out the straight dark mass that fell past her shoulders. She preferred the way it looked in the summer with coppery auburn highlights dancing in it. Everything about the winter seemed dreary and dull, including her hair.

She looked down at her conservative pleated navy skirt and white blouse, deciding to change to jeans and a hoodie before she fixed a can of soup for supper. She was careful with her work clothes. Image was important at most jobs. She really ought to buy some new suits. But she would probably only purchase more of the same. She found herself buying similar style work clothes over and over — boxy jackets with black, brown or navy skirts. All very neat, professional and plain. Just a creature of habit, she supposed. Kim let out a deep sigh and got on with the business of fixing a quick dinner.

Kim was plagued by the feeling that going over to the Gardner house was a mistake. Her intuition in such matters was usually right. Yet she felt compelled to go there and talk to Evelyn Gardner. Helping people was what she did for a living. Helping Mike deal with his difficult personal situation seemed important. He was suffering, and her heart went out to him. Kim hoped there was a chance that Evelyn would listen to reason if approached in the right way. Kim intended to try.

The Gardner house was dark. Odd since Evelyn was supposedly expecting her. Evelyn's car was parked in the driveway, but Mike's wasn't there. Of course, Kim wouldn't have expected it to be. Evelyn would have made certain that Mike and the girls were out. Evelyn wanted this conversation to be a private one. She'd already made that clear.

As Kim rang the doorbell, she realized her palms were sweating. She waited. No sound of anyone within. Maybe Evelyn wasn't home after all. She rang the doorbell again.

Kim was getting ready to leave when she noticed the front door was slightly ajar. She pushed, and the door creaked open. She stepped into the dark foyer.

"Hello?" she called out.

No answer. Kim groped for the light switch she knew was on the side wall. In her mind, a warning screamed: *Get out!* Why wouldn't she listen? Kim knew it was because she cared about Mike.

Kim walked toward the living room with a sense of trepidation. The only sound was the ticking of a large grandfather clock that sat in one corner of the room. Kim glanced around. Then she saw Evelyn—and gasped.

Chapter Seven

There was blood everywhere. Seeing the dead was not new to her, but it never got any easier. Her fingers trembled as she reached into her handbag and pulled out her cell phone. Kim's first thought, as she ran from the house, was to call Mike. She thought better of it and dialed 911. Kim sucked in a deep breath, let it out slowly, then reported what she'd seen. She went to her car and sat until the uniforms arrived. Funny how she couldn't stop shaking.

Determining that Evelyn appeared to have died of a gunshot wound, the two uniformed patrol policemen called for detectives and a forensics team.

"I'm Detective Drew Mitchell," the first investigator said. "I've seen you around. You helped Gardner solve the homicide case at that pool club. You're Gardner's girlfriend, aren't you?" He gave her a once-over followed by a dirty, knowing smile. Kim felt as though slime had been spewed on her.

"Did you kill, Mrs. Gardner?" Mitchell said.

Kim felt chilled and began rubbing her arms. "No, I did not kill her. I just came over this evening because she phoned and said she wanted to talk to me about something."

"Yeah? And what was that?"

"I have no idea, but she made it sound important."

"Seems like you're around a lot when people die."

Kim pulled her coat around her. "I wouldn't know."

"I don't believe in coincidence," he said.

She viewed the policeman with distaste. He had a thin face with a prominent nose and a receding hairline. There was a food stain on his shirt front. But it was his manner that made him repellant, not his looks.

Kim was forced to submit to having her hands examined for evidence of gunshot residue when the forensics team arrived.

"I'm Herb Fitzpatrick," the senior police technician said. He was older than Drew Mitchell His tone was courteous and professional. "I know Mike and Evelyn from way back. Sorry to see things end this way for her." He looked down at Kim's hands. "This won't be painful. I just use this kit and it's over in minutes."

Fitzpatrick's polite manner didn't change the fact that the police considered her a suspect. Kim observed the tech as he cleaned his hands with care then put on disposable gloves. He selected a sample disc labeled right hand from his kit, removed the amber disc holder from the clear vial, exposed the adhesive surface of the disc and pressed it firmly against the palm and back of her right hand until the disc lost its stickiness.

"Okay, now flex your knuckles. Good. Now your palm. Okay, got it."

He repeated the same procedure for her left hand.

"Makes you nervous, doesn't it?" Drew Mathews said. He had a nasty smile.

"I'm not nervous. There's no reason to be. I didn't shoot Evelyn. The test will simply confirm that."

He came closer, and Kim smelled something sour on his breath. She stepped back.

"Truth is this doesn't prove a thing. Smart girl like you would have washed her hands before calling us."

"Detective, I was at work all day. I don't know when Evelyn Gardner was shot, but I have a feeling it was some time ago, most likely while I was helping students at the reference desk at the university library."

He appeared amused. "You think you can figure the time of death? Don't tell me you consider yourself a detective."

Kim folded her hands together. "Reference librarians are detectives of a sort. We search for information."

"Dig around like ferrets?"

She would have liked to smack the smirk from his face. But Kim made it a practice never to be rude to anyone, no matter how deserving they might be.

"We do whatever's needed to help our patrons."

"Would you kill your boyfriend's wife if you thought that was needed?"

She met his probing gaze. "Detective, I have never killed anyone. I believe in nonviolence. May I go now?"

"Just one question. When did you last talk to Gardner?"

"Mike? Not recently," she said. Kim began moving toward her car.

She was grateful when no one stopped her.

Once in her Toyota, Kim turned over the engine and drove off as fast as she dared. Her thoughts were confused. Should she stop at the nearest strip mall and phone Mike? Where was he? He could be working. Where were Evie and Jean? Evelyn had not expected them to be home this evening. Evelyn had wanted to talk with her when no one else in the family would be present. What had Evelyn wanted to discuss? Kim didn't have a clue. She wasn't really clairvoyant. Sometimes visions came to her. Sometimes the dead spoke to her in dreams. But this didn't happen often. She preferred it didn't happen at all. Kim just wanted to be a normal woman leading a quiet, ordinary life. Was that too much to ask?

Chapter Eight

Mike Gardner knew that he would never forget what he'd been doing on certain days in his life. One of those days was 9/11. Another was the day Evelyn died.

Gardner felt bone tired. He'd just finished his shift and was thinking about the drug dealer he'd booked that afternoon, a nasty piece of work if ever there was one. Still, it was a righteous bust. Then his cell rang. He thought it must be Evie checking on what time he'd be picking her up at the high school. He was surprised to hear Bert St. Croix's voice at the other end.

"Mike, you on the road?"

"Yes. What's up?"

"Pull over. I'll explain." He did, and Bert said, "We got the call a little while ago. Word is your wife's dead."

Gardner stared at the traffic going by on the road to his left but didn't see it.

"Are you sure?"

"It's been confirmed."

His heart was beating too fast. "I don't understand. She wasn't sick so far as I could tell."

There was a pause at the other end. "Look, I don't know what I'm allowed to say right now, except Evelyn didn't die of natural causes."

Gardner caught his breath. "I see." How many times had he wished her dead? Gardner felt a sense of guilt.

"Who found her?"

"Kim."

He almost dropped the phone. "Are you sure? How could that be? Kim had nothing to do with Evelyn."

"Mike, I don't know the details. I was ready to go to your house and get the story from Kim, but the captain wouldn't let me. He assigned Drew Mitchell."

"I don't understand. Mitch should have phoned me, told me what was going on."

"He'll call you soon," Bert said. Her voice sounded guarded and that worried him.

"Is Kim all right?"

"I guess so," Bert said. He heard the hesitation in her voice. "I'll find out. Meantime, you better pick up the girls. Got somewhere to take them? You can't bring them home. The house is a crime scene. They'd be traumatized."

Gardner punched the dashboard. "Damn! This is crazy! Doesn't make any sense."

Bert agreed with him. "Pull it together for your girls' sakes." She was the voice of reason, and that was a comfort.

"I'll take Evie and Jean to my brother's house. God, I don't know what to tell them."

"Maybe nothing right now, not until we get the whole story." Her voice was calm, soothing.

"You're right," he agreed. "Bert, thanks."

"No need for thanks. I'll do whatever I can."

Strange, hearing Evelyn was dead really didn't seem to upset him as much as hearing Kim had found Evelyn's body. He worried that Kim would be considered a suspect. He knew she would not have hurt Evelyn. It wasn't in her nature. Kim Reynolds helped people. She didn't harm them. Still, he supposed anyone was capable of killing if pushed too far. And Evelyn had a knack for sticking it to people. He knew that better than anybody. But Kim commit murder? No, he wasn't going there. No way.

Chapter Nine

"Why won't you tell me what's going on? I want to know what facts you've established concerning Evelyn Gardner's death."

Bert St. Croix tapped a pen on Drew Mitchell's hardwood desk. He kept his back turned to her and sifted through some papers. She knew Mitchell wasn't busy, just pretending so he could avoid her.

"Hello, I'm still here and I'm not going away. I want to know what's going on."

Mitchell turned and finally faced her. "Yeah, I heard you. I got nothing to say. You're just another detective like me. You got no part in this. The captain assigned me to the case not you." He got to his feet hitching his pants above a paunch.

"Why so secretive?" Bert was several inches taller than Mitchell and used her extra height to advantage. She wanted him to feel her presence.

"Look, if the captain wants you to know anything, he'll tell you."

"Where's Kim Reynolds?"

"I sent her home. Why—were you planning on asking her out?"

Bert felt like smacking the smarmy, insinuating smile off his face. Instead she placed her hands on her hips and narrowed her eyes. "Just what are you trying to say?"

"Hey, everybody knows you hang out with that slutty blond bimbo who waitresses at the Galaxy Lounge, the one with the big boobs. I didn't know she was a lesbo like you, but I should have guessed it when she wouldn't give me a second glance."

Bert felt the blood pound in her head. She took a deep breath. "So you figure every woman who isn't interested in your crude advances must be a lesbian?" Bert shook her head. "You're such a pig."

"Oink, oink to you. Oh and don't ask me for any favors. I won't be sharing information on this case or any other with you."

"You know what happens to pigs, don't you? They get slaughtered." She turned on her heels and walked away.

"Hey, is that some kind of threat?" His voice trailed after her. "Cause I don't put up with that kind of crap."

"Turd," she muttered.

Bert got out of the office as fast as she could. If she stayed near the creep any longer, she was going to have to punch him in his filthy, stupid mouth. But that was what Mitchell wanted. He knew she was not a favorite of the captain, who'd love an excuse to suspend the only woman of color in the Webster Township Police Department for cause. She wasn't going to provide it. What she was going to do was find out what happened to Evelyn Gardner. That would help her friends and show up Mitchell as well. Much more satisfying.

Chapter Ten

Kim was too tired to think. She sat down on her sofa bed and kicked off her shoes, calling herself all kinds of foolish and stupid for going to the Gardner house. Her intuition had warned her it was a mistake. Why hadn't she listened? But she knew the answer. Deep down inside she'd held the hope that Evelyn would say she was signing the divorce decree and leaving town. It seemed so long ago that Mike had asked her to marry him and she'd accepted. Neither one of them expected Evelyn to turn up and destroy their relationship.

Now Evelyn was dead. What would that mean for Mike and her? Would they be able to put the pieces back together? Kim admitted she still loved Mike. He was very likely the only man she could or would ever want to spend her life with. But was that going to be possible? Was love enough?

Evelyn Gardner had been murdered. Detective Drew Mitchell considered *her* a prime suspect. Who else would the detective consider a suspect?

Kim knew the police always looked at family first when a homicide had been committed. Mike would certainly be high on Mitchell's list.

Kim was saved from further contemplation when the doorbell rang. She let Bert St. Croix in. The big detective strode in, skipped the civilities and said, "That bastard Mitchell wouldn't tell me anything about Evelyn's death."

"He seems to think I killed her," Kim whispered.

"He's stupid as well as being a son of a bitch," Bert muttered.

"I guess he's just doing his job. I did go and find Evelyn's body."

"You just naturally have a gift for finding dead people, girl."

"Not much of a gift. I can think of lots better talents."

Kim jumped as she heard the apartment door open. Then she saw Mike Gardner.

"Looks like Bert and I had the same idea," he said. "What better talent are you talking about?"

"Finding the dead," Bert said.

"Yeah, there is that," Mike agreed.

Kim said, "I'd prefer not to have such a gift."

"I don't know," Bert said. "Maybe we should be utilizing your skills more. Every time there's a missing person we think might be dead, we should just give you some article of their clothing to sniff and send you out."

Kim pursed her lips. "Very funny. However, I am not a dog."

"No, but you sure do catch the scent of dead folks. I'd say you've got something in common with bloodhounds." Bert's tone was only half-joking.

"It's caused me nothing but trouble," Kim said. She sank back onto the sofa. Mike settled in beside her and placed his arm around her shoulders.

Mike said, "Honey, I'm sorry for all the trouble I've caused you."

His gray eyes were soft.

It was almost her undoing. She shook her head, choking back a sudden sob. "It's not your fault. Evelyn phoned me yesterday. She was insistent that I come to your house this evening. She said there was something important she had to discuss with me."

"She didn't say what it was?" Bert asked.

Kim shook her head. "No, I don't have a clue what she wanted to talk about. When I turned her down initially, she became more insistent."

"My guess is that she intended to hit you up for money," Mike said.

Both Kim and Bert turned questioning looks on him.

"What makes you say that?" Bert asked.

"Because she tried to hit me up. She had this crazy idea that she needed plastic surgery out in Hollywood to compete as an actress.

She wanted me to sell the house and give her half of the money. We argued about it."

Bert stood poker straight. "Mike, maybe you better not say anything more."

They exchanged looks. He said, "I didn't kill her."

"Never thought you did. But I wouldn't make that admission to Drew Mitchell. He'll consider it as going to motive."

"I have a bad feeling he already considers both Mike and me suspects," Kim said.

"No doubt," Mike said. "Kim, can you describe what you saw at the house?"

"I hate going through it again." She closed her eyes. "I knocked at the door first. No one answered. But I felt certain that Evelyn was there waiting for me. Finally, I just walked in."

"The door was open?" Bert asked.

Kim looked up at Bert, who had started taking notes on a small black pad. "The door was ajar. I thought she was expecting me and had left it slightly open. But upon reflection I suppose whoever killed her left it that way."

"Were you aware of anyone else in the house?" Bert asked.

Kim shook her head. "No, I don't think anyone else was there."

"So the killer had already left."

"Okay, where was Evelyn's body?" Mike asked.

"She was right there in the living room, crumpled on the floor. There was so much blood. Her eyes were open. The expression on her face was horrible. I felt she must have suffered. I called 911. The uniformed policemen came first. They called it in as a possible shooting. Then Detective Mitchell arrived."

"Kim, this is very important," Mike said. "Did you see a gun?"

She bit down on her lower lip, trying hard to remember everything she'd observed in the room.

"No, I didn't see a weapon of any kind." She paused, closed her eyes, and put herself back into the room, although she hated doing it.

"There was something odd, though. Mike, you know the

drawer you always lock because you keep your spare gun in there? Well, it was open. But it was empty."

Mike exchanged a grim look with Bert. "Since we were issued Glock automatics, I had my old .38 in that drawer. Only a few people knew I kept it there."

"Like Evelyn?" Bert asked.

"Yeah, she knew. I put my Glock and holster away in that same drawer at night. I take it out when I go on duty. She saw me doing it one day and said it made her feel safe."

"She knew where you kept the key?" Bert asked.

Mike gave a slight nod of his head.

"So she could have unlocked it and got the revolver out."

"But why?"

"She might have been frightened," Kim said. "Maybe the murderer phoned and threatened her or maybe a person she feared was at the door."

"Why would she let a murderer in?" Mike asked.

"It might have been someone she knew."

"Someone else she was asking for money?" Bert shot a meaningful look at Mike. "You did say she wanted money from you. She could have been asking other people for it as well."

"But," Kim said, "that wouldn't have necessarily have caused her to be frightened, would it?"

"She could have been frightened if she was trying to blackmail someone," Mike said.

"You knew her best," Bert said. "Would she do something like that?"

Mike's face was taut. "I'm thinking I never really knew Evelyn at all."

Kim silently agreed with him.

Chapter Eleven

Drew Mitchell wasn't happy. His first homicide case and it was turning ugly. He wanted to wrap it up quick. He saw only one way this could play out. The suspects were going to draw a lot of sympathy. He'd be looked at as a villain. He didn't like the idea of being considered a rat by fellow cops. He punched his desk.

"That make you feel good?" Captain Nash studied him.

Mitchell had been alone in the drab room shared by the plainclothes detectives.

"Why don't you come into my office so we can talk?" This Mitchell realized was not a suggestion but an order.

Mitchell followed the captain through the frosted glass door of Nash's private office. He found his superior intimidating. Nash was a big, burly man possessed of homely features. His nose, broken at some indefinite time in the past, had never properly mended and gave him the appearance of a former boxer. Mitchell seated himself across from the captain.

"What's your take on the Evelyn Gardner case?"

"I've started questioning people," Mitchell said. "We have several suspects."

"Like who?"

Mitchell squirmed in the chair and pulled at his shirt collar. "The thing is we both know that most homicides are committed by someone the vic knows. In the case of a woman who dies in the home, it's usually the result of a spousal altercation—husband, boyfriend, significant other. Evelyn was shot to death. We haven't found the weapon yet, but we're searching for it. There's woods around the Gardner house. We're canvassing."

"I'd like to see you wrap this as soon as possible with no screw-ups." Nash's voice was granite hard.

Mitchell swallowed. "Doing my best, Cap."

"Keep me in the loop. Remember, no mistakes." Their eyes met.

Mitchell realized it was what Captain Nash hadn't said that mattered most. A cop's wife had been murdered. The investigation had to be thorough. It had to be a tight fit. Like the captain said: no mistakes. If he was going after Mike Gardner for murder and maybe the Lieu's girlfriend, Kim Reynolds, for conspiracy to commit, there had to be plenty of evidence collected. He'd dig for it like a ferret. This case could make his career if he handled it right. But he was well aware it could detonate like a bomb if he didn't.

Mitchell knew a lot of people in the department thought he was a jerk—like Bert St. Croix. He wasn't any woman's idea of a romantic hero, but he could hold his own. Pity the criminal who underestimated him; pity another cop as well. His jaw set in a grim line.

Chapter Twelve

Bert St. Croix was striding back into the municipal building when she heard voices raised in anger. Curious, she walked in the direction of what sounded like an unpleasant argument. The two men turned out to be none other than Police Chief Sam Morgan and Webster Township Mayor Ryan.

"You've got your police force ticketing my car again. I won't be intimidated by you, Morgan." The beefy mayor was red-faced.

Chief Morgan used his greater height to advantage in dealing with his opponent. "I don't know what you're talking about. You think my people have nothing more important to do all day than follow you around? You're an egomaniac."

"You're a corrupt bully. Don't think people aren't aware of it."

"I'm well-respected in this town, which is more than can be said for you."

"Respect you? No way. Fear you? Absolutely."

"You think you can get rid of me? Fuckin' fat chance! I got a contract."

"Oh, I know you've got a power base, but I think I can show cause for removing you."

Chief Morgan clenched his big hands. "I've seen plenty of you lousy two-bit politicians come and go in my time. You're not the first and you won't be the last. You should go back to doing what you know best, embalming dead people. I think that Gardner's wife is in need of your services. Coroner's Office should be releasing the body soon. You'll feel right at home handling that body, won't you?"

Bert looked intently at the chief. His expression insinuated something that made her wonder. She wanted to hear the mayor's response. But just then, the two men became aware of her presence.

Both of them drew back like prize fighters separating at the bong of the bell for the end of a round. Physically, the chief would have had the advantage. He was older but his body was lean and hard muscled.

"Take good care of that new car," Chief Morgan taunted. "Wouldn't want to see another of your vehicles exploding in the parking lot." With that he moved on.

Mayor Ryan looked apoplectic.

"You all right?" Bert asked.

"That man! How do you stand working for him?" The mayor hadn't expected a response. He hurried away.

Bert was at police headquarters the day the mayor's car had blown up. The car bomb was small, just big enough to ruin the interior of the automobile and send the mayor a message. The chief and the mayor hated each other. Privately, Bert didn't think Mayor Ryan was any match for the wily chief.

She wasn't going to worry about either of them, not when her friends were in trouble. Bert had a bad feeling that Drew Mitchell was planning to make a case against Mike or Kim, maybe both of them. Bert was determined to do everything she could to help her friends—whatever it took. She nodded her head with grim determination.

Chapter Thirteen

Gardner knew the time had come to talk to his children. He conceded that it wasn't going to be easy to tell them that their mother was dead—no not just dead—murdered. He found them in the family room of his brother's house. Evie was working at a desk on a school report while Jean was watching the DVD of a children's movie. In spite of his solemn mood, Gardner smiled when he looked at his girls. He loved them both with his entire being. There wasn't anything he wouldn't do to protect them from harm.

Evie looked up at him. "Dad, when are we going home? I'm missing schoolwork. Why did we come here during the week. Why did we have to stay overnight?" Her sharp mind didn't miss much.

Gardner took a steadying breath. It was time. "There's something I have to tell you. Jeannie, shut off the TV. This concerns you too, all of us as a family."

He was grateful that his brother and sister-in-law were at work and his nephews in school. He needed to be alone with the girls. He led Evie and Jean to the kitchen table, seating himself opposite them so he could look from one to the other. Jean's hair was fair and fine like her mother's had once been, while Evie had honey brown hair and gray eyes that matched his own. They were beautiful children.

"Dad, what's wrong? You've got a weird expression on your face." Evie gave him a worried look. His older daughter was always sensitive to his moods.

"There's no easy way to tell you this. Your mother's dead."

"What?" Evie's expressive eyes opened wide.

Jean said nothing, staring at him as if he'd told her that New Jersey had been invaded by aliens.

"I know it's a shock. It was for me too."

"No, it's not true!" Jean stood up, knocking over her chair.

Gardner reached for her. "Honey, she died at the house. That's why we can't go home for a while."

"She wasn't sick." Jean shook her head in denial.

"She was shot. Someone killed her."

Jean burst into tears. Gardner took her into his arms and comforted the ten-year-old rubbing her back. She still had her baby fat. Such a terrible shock for a child. Of the three of them, Jean was the only one who'd been thrilled that Evelyn had returned. The body of his younger daughter was wracked by sobs.

"I'm not sorry. I wanted her dead," Evie said in a tight voice.

Jean pulled away from Gardner. "How can you say that?"

Evie's face betrayed no emotion. "She was a rotten mother to both of us. Selfish and mean."

Jean blinked with an innocent look. "But Evie, Mom came back to us. She loved us."

"Did she? Did she really? I'm not so certain of that."

"I don't think this is the right time for this conversation," Gardner said. Maybe never. He didn't want to see Evelyn's death destroying the relationship between his two daughters.

"Did she shoot herself?" Evie asked.

"No." Gardner didn't want to say anything more.

"Who would shoot Mom?" Jean asked.

"We don't know that yet, sweetheart."

"But you'll find out, won't you, Daddy?" Jean's trusting, expression tore at his heart.

"I will," he promised, "honor bright."

Gardner kissed each of his daughters on the forehead and held them to him. He was never more aware of the fragility of human life than at this moment.

Chapter Fourteen

"Mitch, they found something."

"In the woods behind the house?"

"Yeah." Herb Fitzgerald moved toward him. Drew Mitchell immediately stood up and came around his desk.

"Murder weapon?"

"Could be," Fitzgerald said.

"Revolver?"

Fitzgerald nodded.

"Prints?"

"Doubt it."

"Get the info back to me fast as possible."

Fitzgerald ran a hand through his thinning hair. "The thing is . . ." Fitzgerald hesitated.

"Go on," Mitchell said impatiently.

"It's a police special. Looks like the ones we used to carry."

Mitchell felt his heart beat faster. The weapon belonged to Gardner. Mitchell knew it. He'd never been more certain of anything in his life. "Run every test you can on that revolver." Everyone thought Gardner was so smart. They called him *the psychologist*. Well, now they were going to find out he wasn't so clever after all. Mitchell licked his thick lips with an air of expectancy. Time to question his main suspect. He was going to break this case fast. He'd have a promotion within the year.

"What have you found out about my wife's death?" Gardner sat down opposite Drew Mitchell.

He felt as if he'd been away from his own desk a lifetime, yet it was only a day. Somehow the office seemed foreign to him as though he'd never seen it before. It was a strange feeling and not a good one, unsettling in fact.

Drew Mitchell gave him a hard stare. "We know your wife took two bullets, first shot was horizontal to the chest. Second one hit her at angle in the back, oriented downward. After she took the first slug, she must have been trying to get away from her killer but when she turned, she fell, and then the second bullet ripped into her."

Mitch removed a bagged revolver from his desk. "We got a ballistics match. Positive I.D. of this as the murder weapon. Look familiar?"

Gardner studied it but made no move to touch the weapon. "It's a .38 caliber Smith and Wesson Chief's Special."

"Like the one the department issued to you?"

Gardner didn't bother to answer what he knew was a rhetorical question.

"Would it surprise you to know that this is the revolver that was used to kill your wife? No answer? Yeah, it's your gun. We found it in the woods by your house where the perp tossed it."

"Any prints?"

"What do you think? A smart perp would wipe his or her prints. The gun was clean."

"That's too bad."

"Yeah, but it won't matter."

"Why not?" Gardner asked, but he was afraid he knew the answer.

Mitch leaned over close to Gardner; his breath stank. "We both know you killed her. You had a girlfriend and your wife got in the way. It's clear as a windowpane."

Gardner's anger stirred. "You might think so, but that's not the case. Your windowpane is in serious need of cleaning."

Mitchell sneered. "Listen, Mike, why don't you just confess here and now? It'll go a lot easier for you. Tell me how you wanted to make her to leave. So you took out the revolver and threatened her. Or maybe she went and got the revolver and threatened you. Yeah, that sounds more likely. You struggled to take the gun away from her and she got shot in the chest. That part was an accident. No premeditation. Come on, Mike, I'll give you your Miranda and you can just confess straight out."

"If I'd killed her, I'd admit it. And I wouldn't have run. I'd have called for an ambulance right off. Happens I had nothing to do with it."

"Then it had to be your girl friend, the librarian. She's the type who keeps it all inside until pow! One day, she just explodes. Typical of those tight-assed gals. She called you and you helped her cover up the murder, right?" Drew Mitchell stared and waited.

"You should write crime novels."

"One of you did it. Maybe you planned it together. Coming down to the nitty gritty: you or her or both of you. Why don't you make it easy on yourself? You'd just be charged as an accessory. Give her up, Mike. Otherwise, she'll blame you. It always happens that way."

Gardner managed a grim smile. "You're really good at this, Mitch. There's only one slight problem. I didn't kill Evelyn and neither did Kim. Neither one of us had anything to do with her death. You can't make a case against us because we're not guilty." Gardner stood up. "Ever consider that someone might have been burglarizing the house. Evelyn could have taken out the weapon to defend herself from an intruder. Then she was attacked."

"Doesn't work. No signs of forced entry."

"Didn't have to be," Gardner said. "Evelyn was expecting company. She probably left the front door open."

"Doesn't make sense. The house wasn't ransacked for valuables. We checked," Mitchell said. He ran his tongue over his teeth.

"I'm on personal leave. My children need me. So if we're through, I'm taking off."

Drew Mitchell rose to his feet as well. "You can go for now, but we're not done. Like the old saying goes: you can run but you can't hide."

Chapter Fifteen

Kim met with Drew Mitchell at Webster Township police headquarters after work. The police detective had phoned her at the university library during the afternoon. She contemplated another meeting with distaste. Root canal would have been preferable. The first interrogation had been unpleasant enough. What would he want with her now?

"I guess you know why I asked you to come down here today." Kim noted that the detective had a toothy smile.

"Not really. I already told you everything I know."

"Not everything, right?" He gave her that dirty insinuating smirk of his that turned her stomach.

Kim suddenly had a sense of déjà vu. She was back in time. The police officers were questioning Ma and her about Carl, implying that they must have known what he intended to do. She realized then that police were not to be trusted. Mike and Bert were different. She could trust them completely. But it seemed as if the rest were like this detective. They assumed the worst.

"What exactly is it that you think I know?" She did her best to keep the irritation out of her voice. Always be civil, she reminded herself. Do unto others as you would have them do unto you. She lived by the golden rule.

He moved closer to her and she found herself backing away. Kim realized it was an intimidation tactic. She wasn't going to let him see her discomfort. She sat up straight in her chair, stiffening her spine.

"You and Gardner planned this together, didn't you? You both wanted to off his wife. He couldn't get rid of her legally so he whacked her."

Kim tried her best to tamp down her anger. Losing her temper would only cause more of a problem. "That is totally ridiculous. If I was involved in a conspiracy to murder Evelyn Gardner, then why on earth would I arrange to find her body?"

"To throw us off? You can account for your time at the time of the murder. But not Gardner."

Their eyes met and held. "Mike was at work."

"Not the whole time. I checked. His house is off by itself. He could have slipped in without anyone being the wiser. He could have shot his ex and left again without being seen. You planned it together, right?"

Kim shifted in her chair, sensing the tension in the police detective. "Mike and I haven't been seeing each other since Evelyn returned. There was no conspiracy, Detective. Your theory is absolutely wrong."

"We'll see about that," Drew Mitchell said with a cocky grin. He pulled a bagged gun out of his desk drawer. "Recognize this?"

Kim stared at the weapon. "Should I?"

"Gardner ever show it to you?"

"Is it his?"

"Don't you know?" he persisted.

"I know nothing about firearms. How would you expect me to identify this weapon?"

"Cagey, aren't you? Answering questions with questions. Maybe you need me to shake you up a little. If you don't turn on your boyfriend, he and you go down for this together. Now do you have something to tell me?"

Kim folded her hands over her chest. "If you investigate further I have a feeling you'll discover that Mike had nothing to do with his wife's death. He's too decent to have harmed her. As for me, I know nothing about it. May I go now?"

"Yeah, but don't leave town."

"I wasn't planning to go anywhere." Although visiting Ma in Florida would have really been nice about now. But that wasn't going to happen any time soon.

Kim left police headquarters and the civic center complex as quickly as she could. The wind whipped across her face. Kim found she could barely catch her breath. Pulling her navy wool coat collar up, she thought how much she hated winter. She supposed it was appropriate that Evelyn Gardner had died in the season of death.

In the parking lot, her Toyota Corolla's engine turned over. She started the heat before fastening her seatbelt. She realized her hands were shaking and not from the cold. She needed to talk to Mike. He couldn't have killed Evelyn no matter what the provocation. No, he wouldn't do it. But someone had murdered Evelyn Gardner, and Kim felt that that person was close by. She sensed the evil.

Chapter Sixteen

Kim phoned Mike as soon as she arrived back at her apartment. "Detective Mitchell questioned me again," she said. "This time he had me come to police headquarters."

"He did the same with me."

"I think we better talk in person."

"No problem. The girls are with my family. I'll meet you at your apartment as soon as I can."

"All right."

While she waited for Mike, Kim fixed herself a can of tomato soup and toasted a slice of whole grain bread. She wasn't hungry but knew she needed to eat. It wouldn't do to starve herself and get sick. She tended to be on the slender side. Well, at least she didn't have to worry about dieting.

She would have liked to pick up a novel to read as she usually did in the evening. Nothing better for her than escaping into a book. But tonight all she could think of was Detective Mitchell's interrogation. He'd played with her like a cat clawing at a bird. She shuddered.

Mike entered the apartment looking solid, his smile reassuring.

"I'm glad you're here," she said.

"I'm glad you're glad."

Mike drew her toward him. This was what she needed and wanted. The physical pull between them was still there, the chemistry powerful. She'd tried for so long to forget, to deny the connection between them. She'd only been fooling herself. Mike kissed her, not a gentle kiss but a deep knowing one full of recognition. They finally came apart, breathless. Neither spoke.

They didn't have to speak to communicate. *He's the love of my life. There will never be anyone else for me but him.* The thought was startling, but she knew it was true.

"I kept the ring," Mike said, caressing her cheek. "It's yours anytime you want it."

"First, we have to get this mess about Evelyn cleared up."

Mike shrugged. "What's a murder between friends?"

Kim frowned. "You can't joke about this."

"Death is too important to take seriously. Care to swap a little spit?" He reached out to kiss her again, but she pushed him away.

"Detective Mitchell believes we conspired to murder Evelyn. That doesn't put me in an amorous mood. I'm worried, Mike, frightened. I don't have a good feeling about him."

"Honey, if he's got me pegged for killing Evelyn, he's on the wrong track. He's a good cop. He's sure to get on the right track. He'll figure that out fast enough."

Kim bit her lower lip. "I respect your insight into people. But sometimes you're a little too optimistic. I don't trust Mitchell. I think he has his own agenda."

"At this point in the investigation, I can't interfere. That would make me appear more suspicious."

"You're already a person of interest in Evelyn's homicide," she pointed out.

"That's why I have to stand back and let Mitch handle it."

"I don't like it one bit. He's looking for evidence against you. He's zeroed in and won't be looking at the whole picture. 'The soul selects her own society, then shuts the door.'"

"That a poem?"

She nodded.

"Didn't know you were a poet."

"I can't take any credit. It's by Emily Dickinson."

Mike leaned over and kissed her again.

"You're distracting me."

"I hope so. That was the idea."

She took his hand in hers. "I'm afraid. I just feel so helpless."

"Honey, we have to let this play out." Mike squeezed her hand. "Get some sleep. Go to work tomorrow and forget all about Evelyn. What I'd like to do is spend the night with you."

"They might have someone watching you."

He nodded. "I need to get back to the girls anyway. I just don't want you to be upset. Promise me you'll try to stop worrying, okay?"

"Easier said than done. But I promise to do my best."

They kissed one last time; then Mike left and she felt bereft.

That night, the old nightmares returned.

Chapter Seventeen

The kid approaching Drew Mitchell had a pimply face. The detective pegged him as maybe sixteen or seventeen. The youth was slim with a concave chest. He looked around with a nervous glance.

"They told me you were the detective investigating that lady's murder, the policeman's wife."

Mitchell said, "That's right. And you are?"

"Gary Jenkins." The boy's Adam's apple bobbed.

"You have some information regarding Evelyn Gardner's death?"

The youth rubbed his hands against the sides of his jeans. "Well, I'm not sure. But I saw the story in the newspaper. They had a picture of the police officer. Well, the thing is I'm pretty positive I saw him one day talking to my old English teacher in the supermarket, and he had a gun in a holster under his jacket that he sort of showed to Miss Reynolds. I got really scared, thought maybe he intended to hurt her. But then he said how he was going to kill his wife. Something about solving his problem."

Mitchell said, "Why don't you sit down and tell me all the details? From the beginning. I'd like to get a complete statement. Can you remember his exact words? It could be important."

The youth swallowed hard again. "I'm not sure, but I'll try."

"Good." Mitchell gave a quick nod of approval. "Take your time."

This was it! A key witness who could toast Gardner. Drew Mitchell smelled a promotion blowing in the wind in his direction and it was sweet and fragrant.

On Saturday morning, Kim was awakened by the persistent ringing of her telephone. She hadn't been sleeping well and felt groggy. Her throat was scratchy; her head ached. She hurried to the kitchen area and grabbed the receiver offering a weary "Hello."

"Kim, it's Bert. I have something important to tell you."

She knew the news was not good by the tone of Bert's voice.

"About Mike?"

There was a hesitation. "He was arrested this morning."

"God, no." Kim's legs started to buckle. She grabbed the kitchen counter for support. "I had a feeling this was going to happen."

"Mike told me you warned him. So did I. He refused to believe it until now. Seems he was blindsided about anything connected with Evelyn."

"What about Evie and Jean?"

"They're still with Mike's brother, his wife and kids."

"I know Mike and his brother are close. That will help."

"Yeah, Chuck seems like a good guy."

"Who arrested Mike?"

"Who do you think?"

"Detective Mitchell."

"You got it. Right in front of Mike's family. I was told he seemed to enjoy it, the bastard."

"It had to be terrible for the girls." Kim thought of how awful it had been when the police came to their house to tell Ma and her what Carl had done.

"Chuck phoned me. Mike asked him to call. Wanted me to phone you too."

"Bert, how can we help him?" Kim took the receiver of the portable phone to her sofa bed and sat down.

"Mike needs a good criminal defense attorney. But they cost a lot, and Mike's not rich. I'm going to ask around who's good."

"I'll do some research too. If you like, I'll go with you to see the lawyer once we find one we think is good."

"Okay. I'll phone you later. I've got something to do first. Then I'll get right on it."

Bert stalked into the office and slammed her fist down on Drew Mitchell's desk.

Mitchell jerked backward. "Christ, what's wrong with you? And what are you doing here anyway. Aren't you off today?"

"You arrested Gardner this morning. Of all the stupid things you could do, that's the worst." Bert didn't shout or curse but she felt like doing both.

"Listen, I've been collecting evidence. This isn't your case so fuck off!"

She had a strong urge to punch the idiot in his face but somehow managed to control herself.

"You know Mike is a smart cop and a first-rate investigator. If he were planning to murder his wife, why would he kill her in such an obvious way?"

"So he's good at his job. But this was personal. Domestic disputes can turn violent. A cop isn't immune."

"Do some more digging. You haven't even got below the surface," she urged.

"Look, I've done my job." Mitchell raised his chin.

"Well, congrats. Must have really gotten off on arresting Gardner in front of his kids. No doubt now you'll get that promotion you've been angling for."

Mitchell's faced colored. "What's that supposed to mean?" His voice was loud and it aroused the attention of others in the office.

"St. Croix, in my office now."

Captain Nash jerked his thumb for emphasis. Bert followed him without giving Mitchell the satisfaction of a backward glance.

"Close the door," the captain said.

Bert did as she was told then folded her arms over her chest bracing herself.

"Mitch was just doing his job. Stop harassing him. Gardner can't be treated different because he's one of us. The rules are the same for everyone. You know that."

Bert stared at the captain's lined face. "Mitch didn't spend enough time collecting evidence."

"Frankly, I don't think there's much evidence to collect. This is cut and dried. Admit it: if Gardner wasn't your pal and sometime partner, you would think just the way Mitch does. You're letting emotion get in the way of sound reasoning."

"You don't respect my judgment," she said.

"You're accusing me of something I'm not guilty of," he replied. His voice was like a gravel pit, the result of years of chain smoking.

"Let me look for some other leads."

"Croix, we have other cases that need your attention."

"I believe we haven't done enough on this case. Give me the opportunity to dig deeper. Sure, someone killed Evelyn Gardner but it wasn't Mike."

"We don't have manpower to waste on a case that's already a wrap."

"What's if it's not a wrap? I don't think it is. I'm going to investigate with or without your blessing. But it would be easier if I could do it officially. Gardner's your best detective. If there's a sliver of hope that he's been arrested by mistake, don't you want to grab for it?"

"Stop pushing, Croix."

Bert stood hands on hips and faced him. "You don't respect my opinion because I'm an African-American and a woman besides."

"Don't pull that crap on me! I'm fair-minded."

"But I wasn't your choice for the job, was I?"

"Crying discrimination is dirty."

"Arresting an innocent man for murder is a lot worse."

They were nose to nose. And then Nash backed down. "Fine, you take a few days to investigate Evelyn Gardner's murder on your own. You'll find out how wrong you are. When you do, I expect you to crawl into my office and apologize. In fact, I'm going to demand it."

"Right." She did her best not to smile.

Chapter Eighteen

The office of Frederick Douglas Lincoln had definitely seen better days, Kim reflected.

She glanced over at Bert, who seemed to be thinking the same thing.

"I checked around," Bert said. "He's got a winning reputation. Even the judges respect this guy. And that's saying something for a defense attorney."

"I didn't say a word," Kim replied.

"Okay, granted the office does look stark—all right, shabby, maybe even seedy."

Kim didn't respond. She glanced at the faded blue wallpaper then looked down at the place in the worn carpeting where someone had ground in chewing gum. There were two battered wooden desks and chairs that appeared to have been left behind by a previous tenant. A single narrow window provided light. When Kim pulled up the ancient blind, she was greeted by a view of a brick wall and a dirty alley.

"Sorry to make you wait," the attorney said, returning from the outer office.

"That's quite all right," Kim said.

He was tall, dark-skinned, well-built and she estimated his age at around thirty-five. He wore a conservative gray wool blend suit, white shirt and blue striped tie. He was dressed professionally, at least. He dropped a legal pad on his desk.

"I need the details of the case," he said.

Bert filled him in.

"I don't usually represent policemen," Lincoln said. "But it sounds as if this one may have been treated unfairly. I'll go talk to him."

"That's great. But just one thing," Bert said. "How come you got such a lousy office? I thought lawyers tried to impress their clients."

"I don't have to impress clients. I keep my expenses down so I can ask for lower fees. I represent a lot of people who barely eke out a living. I also do as much *pro bono* work as I can manage. So, no fancy office, no assistants. You want the pricy people, walk up the block. Plenty of attorneys downtown in the high rent buildings."

Bert gave him a curt nod as if to say he'd do just fine. Kim had formed a similar opinion of the man. Her intuition told her he was good people.

"I'll contact the prosecutor's office first thing Monday morning," Lincoln promised.

"How soon can we bail Mike out?" Kim asked. "He doesn't belong in jail."

"Bail may only be set by a Superior Court judge when there's a charge of murder. Judges have wide discretion in determining the amount of bail to be set in New Jersey." His manner was calm and professional. "There is a bail schedule. But let's go over the factors that can be considered." He ticked them off on his long fingers. "First, the seriousness of the crime, the likelihood of conviction, the extent of punishment prescribed in the statute. Next, the defendant's criminal record and previous record on bail."

"Mike's clean," Bert asserted.

"Okay, that a positive. What about the defendant's reputation and mental condition?"

"He's got a spotless reputation," Kim said. "He's well-respected in Webster Township."

"Good." Lincoln scribbled something on his yellow pad. "Length of the defendant's residence in the community?"

"I believe he's a lifelong resident," Kim said.

Lincoln nodded. "The defendant's family ties and relationships?"

"His home is there and his children go to school in the community," Kim said.

"Another positive. Makes him unlikely to be a flight risk. Okay,

I'll talk to Lieutenant Gardner about the rest: employment status, record of employment, financial condition and the identity of responsible members of the community who will vouch for his reliability."

"Can I see him?" Kim asked, swallowing hard.

"Best you don't try right now. He's in custody at the county jail. It's not a great place. I'll be visiting him as soon as possible. Try not to worry."

Kim appreciated the attorney's words but she had to worry. Jail was the last place on earth Mike Gardner should be, for many reasons.

Chapter Nineteen

"*You up for visiting* the crime scene?" Bert asked Kim.

"Not really, but if it could help Mike I'll go back there."

Bert was driving, which was just as well. Kim would have found it difficult to concentrate on the road. Neither of them spoke much, each lost in thought. When they arrived at Mike's house, Kim let out a deep sigh. She couldn't help remembering how happy she and Mike had once been there together. They'd made love in his house. She had felt herself to be part of a real family for the first time in her life. And then Evelyn had come along and destroyed everything. Even in death the woman was destroying her life and Mike's.

"Let's go inside," Bert said. "I've got the key."

"They're letting you continue the investigation?" Kim was surprised.

"Let's just say I know how to talk the talk."

The last time Kim had been in the living room of Mike's house, his wife had been dead on the floor. Now Kim looked at the room thoughtfully. Her eyes were immediately drawn to the center of the room where chalk marks and brown stains reminded Kim of the bloody corpse. She turned away, feeling sick.

"Try not to think about it," Bert said. "We need to concentrate on finding connections between Evelyn and other suspects. Screw the emotions. Strictly cool logic and reason."

"Right." Easier said than done. "Do you know what we're looking for?"

"You're the finder. Just sniff around a bit."

Kim pursed her lips. "You know I don't like being compared to a bloodhound."

"Okay. But you do have this way of knowing things."

"Sometimes, not always. I don't exactly control it. Let's start in Evelyn's bedroom. And if she used a computer, we should look for emails."

Bert nodded. "I'll look around Evelyn's room. You check for computers. I'm certain Mitch wasn't thorough. He zeroed in on Mike from the start."

Kim went from room to room. Mike wasn't a computer geek. He'd been a marine, she knew, and was more interested in physical activity, even though his mind was sharp. There was gym equipment in the basement, where he worked out.

She found a computer in Mike's teenage daughter Evie's bedroom. It was a good laptop set up on a desk with a printer. Kim woke up the machine. The screen was loaded with icons. Most seemed related to school or music. She clicked a couple, found links to open courseware. Bright girl. She found Evie's email account, but it was password protected which prevented further snooping. If the girl's mother had used this laptop for emails, there was no sign of it. Kim didn't have an email address for Evelyn. She searched desk drawers but found nothing helpful. She would have to ask Evie.

Kim walked to the guest room where Evelyn had been staying, the fourth bedroom in the upstairs of Mike's home. Bert had the drawers open in a walnut dresser.

"Find anything?" Kim asked.

Bert held up eight-by-ten glossy photographs of Evelyn.

"Nice."

"Part of a fancy professional portfolio."

Kim studied the photos. "Very flattering."

"I guess she thought a lot of herself. Big ego."

"Anything here that might prove useful?"

"Not really. Some nice clothes, perfume, make-up and a few expensive-looking pieces of jewelry. Here's a cute little designer number." Bert held up a pair of faded jeans with holes cut in the knees as well as some provocative locations. "Look at that designer label. Would you believe Evelyn bought stuff like this?"

"Maybe Evelyn wanted to look hip when she went to audition for acting roles."

Bert shook her head. "Where I come from, people who are poor do their best to avoid looking it. One case I had in Bed-Stuy, a kid killed another for an expensive pair of sneakers."

"Couldn't he just steal them?"

"He did—at knife point. Trouble was the vic made the mistake of objecting."

Kim furrowed her brow. She didn't understanding that kind of thinking. She'd never intentionally hurt anyone in her entire life and never considered stealing anything.

Bert lifted a hot pink silk shirt. "Another designer label. So I guess Evelyn wasn't as broke as she claimed." Bert smiled cynically.

"We did think she was taking advantage of Mike's generosity," Kim observed.

"Yeah, the bitch was scamming him for sure."

"Is there anything useful?" Kim glanced around the room.

"More interesting is what's not here."

Kim tilted her head. "Like what?"

"Like a cell phone."

"Maybe Detective Mitchell found her phone and took it."

"Nope, I looked at what was listed as being taken into evidence. No cell."

"The murderer could have taken it."

"It would be the smart thing to do," Bert agreed. "Lot of people text. All kinds of interesting messages might be on her cell. We'd also have had her phone list."

"I think we need to talk with Evie," Kim said. "She's a smart girl. There's a chance she'd have some information that would help us."

"Okay, let's find out where Chuck Gardner lives."

Kim volunteered, "Mike keeps his address book in the nightstand next to his bed," then felt her face grow hot and flushed.

Bert gave her a knowing look. "Don't be embarrassed. You and Mike were going to get married before that bitch showed up. It doesn't surprise me that you slept together. Now let's get a look at the address book."

It felt strange being in Mike's bedroom again. Kim glanced around. It was such a Spartan room, so masculine, just like Mike. The scent of him lingered. What she wouldn't give to feel his strong arms around her once again, loving, reassuring. But she needed to be the strong one now. He needed her help, hers and Bert's.

"Got it," Bert said. She held the small black book up with a smile of triumph. "I'll phone Chuck."

They were almost at the front door when they heard a noise at the back.

Kim and Bert exchanged looks. Kim knew Bert wanted her to remain still. They listened to the sound of glass shattering. Bert snapped open her holster, pulled her Glock and gestured for Kim to stay put. Kim gave a silent nod. Bert moved toward the kitchen with the grace of a panther.

Kim heard the sounds of a struggle and a man's indignant yelp. A few minutes later, Bert returned with a handcuffed male who she shoved none too gently in front of her.

The man turned to Kim. "Hey, if this Amazon's your partner, you better tell her to cut out the rough stuff. I got rights."

"Listen asshole, I informed you I was a police officer. You need to quiet down."

"You could have broken my arm. And you didn't have to cuff me. I'm a law-abiding citizen."

"I need to see some I.D."

"My inside pocket."

Bert pulled out the man's wallet, looked at the picture on his driver's license and then at the man himself. "You Richard Jameson?"

"That's right. Most people call me Rick. That's my professional name, Rick James."

"Long way from L.A., Rick. What are you doing breaking into a policeman's house in New Jersey?"

The man swallowed and looked down at his shoes. "I wasn't

exactly breaking in. I was looking for Evelyn. I was supposed to meet her here. When there wasn't any answer to my phone calls, I figured she was trying to avoid me."

Bert raised her brows. "And why would that be?"

"She owes me money. I wanted to collect on it."

"But you know she's dead, don't you?"

The man looked surprised. Kim thought the surprise was genuine. "No, I didn't know."

"You don't read newspapers?"

"I just flew in from L.A. We don't get your local yokel news out there."

"So how did you know Evelyn Gardner?"

"She and I go way back. We're both actors—*were* both actors. We've had bit parts, walk-ons, been extras, but neither one of us scored a breakthrough. We were both nearly broke. Evelyn borrowed some money from me. Said she needed it to get back home. Claimed people here owed her. Said her old man would give her what she needed to keep her career going. If I loaned some cash, she said she'd be able to pay me back when she returned and even help me out."

Bert looked Jameson up and down. Kim did as well. He was relatively good-looking. He had good hair, a cleft chin, was trim and dressed fashionably in designer jeans and a quality leather jacket. "So pretty boy, were you sleeping with Evelyn Gardner?"

"That's none of your business."

"I think it is, since someone murdered her. It could be you."

Jameson shook his head. "No way! Evelyn and me were friends, good friends. I wouldn't hurt her."

"Did she use a cell phone to call you from here?"

"Evelyn didn't bother to phone me after she left L.A."

"You know who she was going to see when she got here besides her husband? She talk about any old friends?"

Jameson hesitated, but then shook his head. "No, she was private, kept her plans close."

Kim had a sense that he was lying but decided to hold her tongue. This was Bert's show.

"Are you going to arrest me?"

"Where are you staying?"

"The Quarters Motel . . ."

"Plan to be here a while?"

"I'm not sure there's much point, now that Evelyn's—"

"But there *is* a point," Bert said. "You can go home when I say you go home. If I want you and you aren't around, I'll have the L.A, cops haul you in. You not only broke into a cop's house, you broke into a crime scene, a murder scene to boot." Bert uncuffed him. "You understand, honey?"

"I told you everything. I don't know anything else."

"Maybe you'll think of something. What flight did you come in on? When did it arrive? Did you rent a car or come out here by taxi?"

As he responded, Bert took notes, then walked Jameson out to his rental car and saw him off.

"What do you think?" Kim asked.

"Yon Cassius had a lean and hungry look. I think he knows more than he's telling us."

"But you didn't arrest him."

"He'd get bail and be gone." Her face hardened. "This way he may stick around."

Kim didn't envy Jameson. He didn't know it yet, but Bert could be relentless. And finding out who murdered Evelyn Gardner was her top priority.

Bert said, "I want to talk to Mike's daughter, Kim. Evie may be able to help us."

Chapter Twenty

When Evie saw them in the doorway of her uncle's house, she ran to Kim and hugged her. Then the girl burst into tears. Kim held her close.

Bert's heart ached for the girl and her loss. She remembered what it was like to lose her own mother. Of course, her mother had been a warm, caring person very different from Evelyn Gardner.

Around her sobs, the girl told Kim, "I'm sorry I said all those mean things to you. But you shouldn't have walked away from Dad. He loved you, needed you, and he still does."

Bert watched Kim pat Evie on the back in a comforting gesture. "I couldn't get in the middle between your parents. It would have been wrong. But Bert and I are going to help your father."

Evie looked from Kim to her. "Hi, Bert. They're saying awful things about my dad, that he murdered Evelyn." Bert observed that the girl had mentally distanced herself from her mother by speaking of *Evelyn* rather than *Mom*.

Bert said, "Evie, I have some questions I need to ask you."

"Sure, anything that could help Dad."

"Why don't we sit down, okay?"

Evie led them into the family recreation room. Evie's Aunt Louise, a plain, nondescript woman on the plump side, offered to make everyoone hot chocolate and left them alone. Bert settled into a comfortable chair while Kim joined Evie on an overstuffed leather sofa.

"So what did you want to ask me?"

Evie looked more like her father than her mother. She had his gray eyes, but her face was heart-shaped, her lips fuller, and her hair honey brown.

"Evie, did you ever see your mother using a cell phone?"

The girl frowned at her. "Don't call me Evie anymore. I don't like that name. It's really *her* name. I want to change it." She turned to Kim. "I want to do what you did."

Bert shot a quizzical look at Kim. "You changed your name?"

Kim shrugged. "Long story. Short version: I didn't want to be Karen Reyner anymore. My supposed father, Carl, murdered some people at the V.A. He was a troubled individual. He and I never got along. I guess I felt the need to distance myself from him. I decided to reinvent myself. The name change was symbolic."

"Well, I want to do it too. I want to legally change my name." Evie lifted her chin.

"When your father is released, you can talk that over with him," Bert said.

Evie gave her a mutinous look.

"Bert's right," Kim agreed. "I'll help you with it if you like, but right now let's concentrate on your father's problem." Kim's eyes expressed compassion, kindness and understanding. It seemed to work with the girl. She gave a curt nod.

"Okay," Evie said. "There's nothing more important than proving Dad isn't guilty. I guess everything else can wait."

Bert was becoming impatient. She needed to get the girl focused. "What about the cell phone? Did your mother use one?"

"Yeah, all the time."

"Do you know where she kept it?"

Evie glanced upward in an expression of concentration. "I guess in her bedroom. But she mostly had it with her."

Kim gave Bert a meaningful look. They'd searched the house thoroughly. They hadn't found a cell phone. To Bert it suggested that the murderer had taken the phone because his or her number was listed on it. There could have been incriminating text messages as well.

"Did your mother use your computer?"

"Maybe, but not when I was home." Evie's expression was thoughtful.

"Did she set up an email address on your machine?"

THE BAD WIFE

Evie licked her upper lip. "I don't know. I don't think so."

"But you don't know for sure?" Bert pressed.

"I'm sorry. I'm no help am I?" A fat tear rolled down the girl's cheek.

Kim squeezed Evie's hand. "You're trying to help. That's what matters."

Evie abruptly stood up. "I'll tell them I killed her. I hated her enough. I'll say it in court. Then they have to let Dad go."

Kim rose beside her. "Honey, your dad wouldn't want you to lie."

"I could have done it. She was so awful. Even Jeannie was finally catching on." Evie's voice grew louder, more intense.

"You were in school at the time your mother was killed," Bert said in a flat tone of voice. "That can easily be verified."

Evie's face flushed with color. "Well, Dad was working, wasn't he? What's the difference?"

"I've checked. The medical examiner places time of death when your father wasn't at his desk or out on a call. It was his lunch hour. Your dad says he was taking a walk in the park while eating a sandwich he'd brought with him. No one saw him."

"I make our sandwiches every morning," Evie said. "Dad says I make great lunches."

"I'm sure you do," Kim said. Bert thought she detected tears in Kim's eyes.

Bert decided not to push too hard for answers the girl probably didn't have. Evie was in a fragile state.

"Is there anything else?" Evie asked.

"Not right now," Bert said.

Louise Gardner returned with mugs of hot chocolate and oatmeal cookies. Her presence eased the tension in the room. They all sat together for a while, shared the snack, and talked about nothing more significant than the weather.

As they left, Kim turned to Bert. "What do you think?"

"I'm going to take a look at Evelyn's actor pal."

Kim said, "I think we have to talk to Mike as well. He might have some ideas."

Bert agreed. There were answers out there. It was just a matter of finding the right questions.

Chapter Twenty-One

The jail was depressing. The brick building, set in a field off Route 130 without fence or sign to identify it, was usually the first place a person in custody was sent. The barred windows were bare, the sooty brick unadorned. The interior was just as dreary: locked doors leading to a long line of steel cages.

Lincoln never liked visiting the jail and never got accustomed to it no matter how many clients he met here. He'd represented many accused criminals but never before a policeman, let alone one accused of murder. He knew he could handle a murder trial, if it came to that, but trying to get a cop off would be a novelty.

Michael Gardner looked as gray as the walls.

"I guess you're the attorney Bert sent to represent me."

Lincoln introduced himself. Gardner's expression was wary.

Lincoln said, "With your permission, I'll be representing you at the bail hearing. I put in the motion on Tuesday. It'll be heard by the judge in Superior Court on Friday."

"I haven't even signed a retainer agreement yet," Gardner said.

"Your friends retained me. I've already spoken to the D.A.'s office. They're asking for Murder One. They're demanding a million dollars in bail. They have it stated on the arrest warrant. I'm fairly certain I can talk the judge into seven hundred and fifty thousand."

Gardner pushed out a raspy breath. "I didn't kill my wife. I want you to know that. I'm not guilty."

"That how you want to plead?"

"You got it." Gardner looked at him with a steady gaze.

Lincoln was skeptical. He heard clients say they were innocent all the time, even the most guilty ones. "I'm certain we could work out a deal if you decide to accept a plea."

Gardner's face tightened. "No deal. I didn't kill her. I know you're used to criminals who cop a plea, but that won't work here."

"All right. Then suppose you tell me everything."

Gardner gave a curt nod. "Just one thing. I'll be the one paying your fees."

"Well, you're a lucky man in one respect."

"How do you figure?"

"You got two pretty women in your corner."

Gardner smiled for the first time. "Yeah, they're both great."

"The lady cop," Lincoln said, "she married or anything?"

"Nope, unattached."

Lincoln flashed pearly teeth. "Good to know. She's a tall drink of water. Lotta woman."

"That she is."

"She's working your case, Gardner."

"Also good to know."

Lincoln had a feeling about this client. The cop seemed straight. Helping the ones that were innocent was what mattered to him. It kept him going.

"Okay, let's get started," Lincoln said, pulling his legal pad out of his briefcase. "We got a lot to talk about."

"When do I get to see Mike?" Kim tried to keep the anxiety out of her voice.

Frederick Douglas Lincoln shuffled some papers around on his desk. She realized he was avoiding her gaze.

"You don't," he said.

"Why not?"

He cleared his throat. "Well, in the first place, Lieutenant Gardner has been placed in administrative segregation."

"I don't understand." She hated it when people used verbal obfuscation. "What does that mean?"

For the first time, the attorney looked her in the eye. "He's in solitary confinement."

Kim gasped. "Isn't it bad enough that he's been accused unjustly?"

Lincoln raised his hands in a gesture of placation. "It's for his own protection. There's people in that facility would kill your friend soon as look at him."

"I should still be able to visit with him."

"Family visits are pre-arranged. We can arrange for a relative to see a prisoner usually once a month. You're not a relation, are you?"

"I'm a good friend."

Lincoln steepled his fingers. "Let me be frank with you. The prosecution is going to contend that Michael Gardner murdered his wife because she was being difficult about a divorce. They will say he was impatient to start a new life with you and that Evelyn Gardner stood in the way. If the prosecution doesn't subpoena you, I don't even want you to be present in the courtroom if we go to trial. Your being there would only help convict Mike."

Kim bit her lower lip and lowered her eyes. "I only want to provide support for Mike."

"I'll tell him that when I see him next."

"When will that be?"

"On Friday. I'm going to make an effort to have Lieutenant Gardner's bail reduced and get him out of the county facility. I believe I can make a strong enough case so that we'll have him out soon."

"That would be great. I realize he's not safe in there."

"No," Lincoln agreed, "he's not."

The lawyer's expression was grim.

Kim let herself hope that Lincoln would get Mike released. The hope gave her something to hang onto.

Chapter Twenty-Two

He was staring at the blank wall thinking how crappy it was that the cell didn't even have a window. And then they came to get him.

"On your feet," the first guard said. He was a big, ruddy-faced man with a large gut that protruded over his pants. He wore a mustache that emphasized an aquiline nose.

"Where are you taking me?" Neither guard bothered to answer. They shackled Gardner's hands and feet so he was forced to shuffle awkwardly from the cell. He was soon joined by two other prisoners. One man, who looked Latino, short and thin, wasn't shackled. The second, who resembled a moose, was shackled like Gardner. This prisoner was taller than either of the guards and broader in build with a shaved head and snake tattoos all over his neck and bulging biceps.

They were led to a large room that served as a communal shower. "You guys got it all to yourselves. Romerez, if you hadn't vomited all over yourself, you wouldn't be this lucky," the correction officer who had spoken to Gardner said. "Since you did, you get the privilege of bathing with two guys up for first degree murder. That one's a cop who offed his wife." The officer pointed an accusing finger at Gardner. "Even better, this one's got a whole string of serial killings. He just loves hookers, don't you, Williams, you sick fuck."

The big man growled at the guard as if he were a rabid dog. The two corrections officers laughed. It was clear to Gardner they enjoyed baiting prisoners.

A third of the room consisted of shelves behind a fence, from which inmates' clothes and towels were exchanged; another third consisted of rows of benches separated by a chest-high partition laced with cubbyholes. The final third was the communal shower, a cement floor with many drains, and four rows of pipes suspended about eight feet above the floor with showerheads jutting out of both sides of each pipe down their entire length.

Once Gardner and the big guy were unshackled, he stripped off his faded green jail uniform. The water was cold when it hit him, but he was grateful to get clean. After a minute Williams dropped his soap and bent to pick it up. Gardner laughed and looked away. A man Williams's size didn't have to worry about unwanted sodomy.

"Watch out!" It was the small man, Romerez, who called out a warning.

Gardner whirled in time to see Williams lunging at him with a sharpened shank of what had once been a spoon. Gardner managed to dodge the blow, and the big man's momentum carried him on, skating across the wet floor and crashing onto his back. Romerez was calling for the guards.

Mike Gardner stood and waited.

The guards arrived but seemed to be in no hurry to check out the situation. They walked into the shower. Williams was still on his back. He flicked the shank away.

"Can't even trust you guys for a second, can we?" the officer with the mustache said in disgust. Then he kicked Williams hard in the stomach.

The prisoner grunted. "You said he's a cop. I hate cops," Williams said through gritted teeth.

The second guard kicked Williams in the groin for good measure. "Likely stuck the damn thing between his butt cheeks."

"Yeah, a real asshole," the other guard agreed. They laughed together.

Gardner wasn't smiling. Neither was Romerez nor Williams, who looked from Gardner to Romerez with the eyes of a stone killer. He made a slashing gesture with his index finger across his throat. Romerez flinched.

Gardner turned to the Latino. "Thanks," he said. "You likely saved my life."

Romerez nodded, then took a fearful glance back at Williams.

* * *

On Friday, Gardner was transported to Superior Court for the hearing on his bail motion.

While he waited in the basement, the place the corrections officers referred to as the "bullpen," Juan Romerez was brought in.

"So we're both up for bail motions today," Gardner said.

"Yes, but I don't have much hope." The younger man sighed. "I just want you to know, I didn't embezzle the money they claim I stole from the company."

Gardner looked at his companion, sizing up the slighter man. "Juan, I'm the last person you need to convince."

"But you are a policeman. Maybe you know someone who will listen to me. I tell the public defender they send me I am not the one who took the money. He tells me to admit my guilt and take the offer the district attorney has given. I tell him no way. I want a jury trial and then he gets angry. If I was guilty of this crime, I would have the money to pay a lawyer of my own choosing. Why does he not see this?"

Gardner was thoughtful. "My partner tells me the lawyer she got for me is good. You got any money to pay an attorney?"

"Very little. Like I say before, if I had stolen the money, then I could pay for the best attorney."

Gardner lowered his head. "When my lawyer comes I'll ask him to talk to you. Maybe we can work something out."

"Thank you. They think because I am Dominican I must be a criminal. I tell them I am an accountant, not a drug dealer."

Gardner had read somewhere that accountants were thieves who stole with pens instead of guns but decided to keep that nugget to himself.

"I figure your warning saved my life. I owe you large."

Chapter Twenty-Three

"So Lincoln managed to get you released on bail," Bert said with satisfaction.

"I had to put up the house, but at least I'm out of that place for now."

"What do you think of your attorney?"

"He'll do. Yeah, he seems okay. He argued that I wasn't any kind of flight risk and that I was no threat to the community. What worries me is that he didn't question the strength of the state's case."

They were sitting in the living room of his brother Chuck's home. Gardner had phoned Bert and asked if she could come out.

"Word is that as defense attorneys go, he's one of the best," Bert said.

"He likes you too. He asked if you're attached. When I told him you weren't, he smiled—more like a broad grin."

"Yeah, well, he's okay, but I don't think it's a good idea for me to be involved with him."

Gardner studied her closed expression. "You mean right now or never?"

"Don't distract me. I need to stay focused. I have some more stuff to go over with you."

"Sure. Ask away."

Bert flipped open her small black notebook and clicked her pen. "Evie said her mother used a cell phone all the time. Kim and I searched your house but didn't find it. We think the murderer might have snatched it."

"Logical assumption," Gardner agreed.

Bert leaned forward. "We also found that the only computer in your house is located in Evie's room."

"True. I'm not much for computers. I have to use one at work and that's enough for me. Jean's allowed to share Evie's computer."

"What about Evelyn? Did she have a computer?"

"No, she didn't have one that I know of."

"She use Evie's computer?"

Gardner thought for a moment. "Can't say I ever saw her go into Evie's room. Then again, I was at work most of the time and she was in the house by herself a lot."

"I talked to Evie about this, but I'm not certain I dug deep enough."

"She's in the rec room with Jeannie and her cousins. I'll get her."

Gardner walked into the recreation room. His two nephews were playing a video game. Jean was watching a TV program. Evie wasn't there. He found her upstairs in the bedroom she and Jean were sharing. Evie was writing in her diary but quickly closed it when Gardner entered the room.

"Dad, you startled me."

"Sorry, I should have knocked. The thing is Bert's here and wants to talk with you."

"Again?" Evie frowned. "There isn't much I can tell her."

He crossed the room and patted her hand. "That's all right. You never know what small detail could prove helpful."

"Dad, are you okay?" Evie's scrunched her face. "I mean you were in jail. That had to be terrible."

"It was. But I'm a tough guy. I can handle it. Still, let's make sure I don't have to go back there."

"Sure, Dad. I love you."

Gardner hugged his daughter and kissed her cheek. "Ditto." He mussed her hair and she gave him an indignant shove. "Ready? Let's talk with Bert."

Bert was pacing the living room.

"Evie's here to help us," Gardner said.

He and Evie sat together on the couch. Bert turned to the girl, dark eyes intense.

"We talked before about whether or not your mother ever used your computer," Bert said.

"Sure, but I don't know if she did."

"The thing is, Kim and I didn't find any personal stuff lying around. Do you know if your mother used a smart phone?"

"No, I didn't get a good look at her cell. She liked her privacy. To tell the truth, I avoided her as much as possible. It was kind of a mutual aversion."

Bert leaned forward. "Okay. But she would have needed to pay for her phone bill. Could she have done an automatic wire transfer of her bills? If so, did you ever see a credit card? We didn't find her wallet either. There's a chance that Evelyn used your computer, Evie. I need your email address and password."

"Sure, no problem." Evie rose, went to a desk and found pen and paper. She wrote out the information and then handed the paper to Bert.

"Okay, this could help. Do I have your permission to borrow your computer?"

"Of course, like I can't use it now anyway, can I?"

"There's tech people who can examine the computer and maybe find out who else has been using it and what messages are there, even deleted ones."

"Sound good," Gardner agreed. "What can I do to help with the investigation? It's my life on the line after all."

Bert's lips narrowed. "You can't. But trust me, I'm going to get answers."

"I'm trusting you with my life," Gardner said.

Chapter Twenty-Four

Kim hadn't fully adjusted to returning to the university as a reference librarian in the humanities library. However, she had a strong sense of being back where she belonged. If only Mike could be proven innocent of killing Evelyn, then everything would be fine.

There was a knock at her apartment door and she went to answer it. "Who s there?" she called out.

"Take a guess."

She unlocked the door as fast as she could and hurled herself into Mike's arms. "Thank God!"

"You need a dead bolt on that door," he said as he nuzzled her ear. "Garden apartments on the ground floor aren't safe without them."

"This is a good area. Low crime."

"Oh, that's right, no burglaries only murders in this neighborhood." He came inside, arms around her, and shut the door. "What about rapes? Any of those around here?" Mike gave her a comic leering look.

"None that I know of. Should I worry?" She was just a breath away from him.

"Yeah, I think you should be worried. I've been in jail. You know how horny guys get there?" Mike ran his hands down her arms and she felt a charge of electricity.

"You weren't there all that long," she said.

"Funny, it seemed like forever."

He pulled her against him and kissed her. It wasn't a gentle kiss but deep and hard, full of pent-up passion. She melted. The kiss lasted until they were out of breath.

"Been a while," he said. "Missed you a whole lot."

"Me too," she managed to say in a small voice. "Why don't you sit down? Take off your jacket. It's so cold out there. Let me get a hot drink."

"Don't want anything but you," he said and pulled her down next to him on the sofa.

"Okay. Did Bert update you on how she's investigating Evelyn's murder?"

"She did."

"Your lawyer, Mr. Lincoln, told me I should stay away from you."

Mike frowned. "I don't see that it makes a difference."

"I guess if the case goes to trial, it'll look bad."

"I'm hoping it doesn't get that far."

"Me too," she said. "I hate the idea of being labeled *the other woman*."

"As far as I'm concerned, you're the only woman." Mike leaned over and kissed her again, a lingering kiss that made her lips tingle. Then he stood up, unzipped his bomber jacket and reached into the inside pocket to bring out his cell phone. She watched as he shut it off.

"Do the same with yours," he said.

Kim went to her handbag and dug around for her cell. She switched it off, then turned off her land phone.

"So what do you have in mind?" She smiled at him, knowing exactly what he intended.

"As that great philosopher anonymous said, *carpe diem*."

"Trying to impress me with your erudition?"

His hands took hers. "Did I succeed?"

"Absolutely." She snuggled into his arms and looked up at him. "Mike, I'm so sorry about this mess."

His eyes were bright with feeling. "Hey, it is what it is."

"Ah, you're waxing philosophical again."

"What I'm really thinking is how hot you are and how I don't want to waste another moment talking when we can be making love."

"Works for me," she said.
"You like a man of action?"
"I do indeed."

Chapter Twenty-Five

Bert decided after talking with Mike and his daughter Evie that the only good lead she had to finding Evelyn's murderer was Rick James as he called himself. The actor was staying at a rundown motel on Route One outside of New Brunswick.

Day had quickly become evening. The desk clerk at the motel had bags under his eyes.

"I'm looking for a Richard Jameson," she said. "He may call himself Rick James."

The desk clerk shrugged. "No one by that name staying here."

She flashed her badge.

The man glanced down at his register. "In B406."

"He in there now?"

"Don't know."

Bert followed the signs and found the room. She knocked, got no answer, tried again and got no response. She went back and got the unhappy desk clerk to come with her and open the door.

"I'm not supposed to do this."

"Yes, you are. I'm investigating a homicide."

The clerk produced a pass card and opened the door.

Jameson was face down on the floor, a pool of blood congealing around him. The clerk standing just behind her gasped. She turned and told him, "I'll make the call. You can go back to the front desk."

The clerk shook his head. "Things like this don't happen here."

"Wrong. They can happen anywhere to anyone."

Richard Jameson wasn't going to be any help after all.

Bert realized she wasn't feeling much of anything and wondered when she had become callous. Shouldn't she be feeling sorrow at the death of another human being? Instead as the stench of death filled her nostrils she felt a sense of disgust. Jameson had known something but hadn't told her when he had the chance. Now he was dead. She felt like kicking his worthless body.

Drew Mitchell showed up with a full forensic team in less than twenty minutes. Bert was waiting for him outside the room.

"How come you didn't tip me off to this Jameson guy before?" Mitchell demanded.

Bert straightened and stood tall, hands on hips. "Would you have cared? All your efforts are geared to proving Gardner's guilt."

"Still are," Mitchell agreed. "How do I know he didn't kill Jameson too?"

Bert felt the anger pounding in her head as she followed Mitchell back to Jameson's motel room. "That's a load of crap and you know it!"

"Do I? I don't think so. Gardner's out on bail. Far as I'm concerned he's a danger to the community. I'm going to see what I can do about sending him back to jail."

"Jameson maybe knew who the killer was. Could be he was blackmailing that person. Jameson was Evelyn's boyfriend in L.A. She could have confided in him."

"He could have been another witness against Gardner," Mitchell said.

"You're a dumb asshole."

Mitchell's face turned red. "Don't know how Gardner worked with you. Maybe he put up with your smart mouth but I'm not going to. Get out of here! This is my case. I don't want or need your interference."

Bert left. She supposed that speaking her mind had made things worse for Gardner. Then again, how could they be much worse?

● ● ●

Early Monday morning, Captain Nash barreled out of his office and loomed over Bert's desk.

"My office now."

Bert looked over and sure enough there was Drew Mitchell sitting way back in his chair a big smirk on his face. So the rat had complained about her. She took a deep breath, let it out slowly and stalked into the captain's den.

"Close the door behind you."

She did as he ordered and waited. He seated himself behind his desk but didn't invite her to sit down. She folded her arms over her chest and waited.

Nash slammed his fist down on the desk. "Damn it! Why did you have to insult Mitch in front of the forensics team?"

Bert stood her ground. "Because he really is a shithead. I used restraint in dealing with him, believe me I did. You realize he's decided that Gardner is guilty of murdering both Evelyn and Jameson? He intends to throw Mike back in the slammer."

She stared at Nash directly and he was the first to look away.

"First of all, you're too militant for your own good. You've been warned about that before. I don't expect you to become diplomatic or teach a course in public relations, but show a little common courtesy to your fellow officers. And no more nosing around. This is not your case. There's work for you to do. I have your new case load in front of me." He handed her a thick folder. "These files need your immediate attention."

She stared at the large pile of folders. "You can't be serious."

"You intend to continue working here, you do the job we pay you to do. Understand?"

"Can't you cut me some slack on this? Gardner is your best detective. You can't deny that. You know the guy better than I do and longer. You know he's not guilty."

Nash looked down, his crooked nose more prominent. "Orders came from above. It's my job if I ignore them. Start working these cases. Leave Mitch to do his job without interference."

Bert snatched up the folder and left the captain's office. The man was close to retiring. He wasn't going to let anything get in the way of his pension.

Drew Mitchell pretended not to see her, fixing his eyes on his computer screen. Bert dropped the files on her desk and left the office. She was furious and didn't trust herself to say so much as a single word to Mitchell. She had to calm down and think through what to do next. There was only one person she could trust to help her do that.

Chapter Twenty-Six

Kim spent a busy morning helping students with their research. Several professors also required her assistance. It was a good thing she wore comfortable shoes because she kept on the move.

Don Bernard visited her. "It's a delight to see you working here again." He was dressed in a cable knit sweater over a blue shirt that accentuated his sky-colored eyes.

Rita joined her at the reference desk. "How can we help you, Dr. Bernard?"

"I'm working on a new book of Renaissance literary criticism. Just dropped by to scope out some sources." He turned on the charm with a dimpled smile. "You ladies do such a wonderful job."

Kim saw Rita return the smile in contrast to her usual sour expression. As Don Bernard walked away, Rita let out a deep sigh. Kim decided that Professor Bernard probably flirted with every woman. It was his nature. He loved women and they adored him. She conceded to being fond of him as well. But he was not the man she loved. She thought of the night she'd spent in Mike's arms and allowed herself a smile of satisfaction.

Kim was putting away some ready reference books when she caught sight of Bert striding across the floor. She could tell something was wrong.

"Can you take a break?" Bert said. "Somewhere we can talk privately?"

Kim signaled Rita that she was leaving. They took the stairs down to the café which was at the basement level. It didn't have the charm of a commercial coffee house but for the campus it was fine. They took a table in the back corner.

"Coffee?" Kim asked.

Bert shook her head. "Maybe later."

"What's happened?"

"I thought with your psychic ability you might already know."

Kim ignored the sarcasm. "You give me too much credit."

"I went to question Richard Jameson. Found him dead. Knife wounds."

Kim's heartbeat quickened. "God."

"Yeah. I should have pressed him harder when I had the chance."

Kim rubbed her forehead. "Evelyn wanted money. She was pushing Mike to sell the house. She might have tried to extort money from someone . . ."

"And that person killed her? Maybe Jameson tried to demand money from that same person."

"Did you get to look around Jameson's motel room?"

"Again, no cell phone or computer," Bert said. "I couldn't do a thorough search of the place. I had to call it in. Drew Mitchell showed up. As soon as he found out the guy was connected to Evelyn he made the assumption that Mike killed Jameson. He wants to put Mike back in jail."

Kim's eyes widened. "He can't go back to that jail. It's too dangerous."

"Captain Nash dumped a shitload of work on my desk. He won't allow me to continue on the murder investigation."

"Why? I thought he was all right with it."

Bert lowered her gaze. "Mitch complained about me. I lost my temper with him."

Kim felt sick to her stomach.

"I need your help," Bert said.

"Of course. But I'm not a trained investigator—"

"You have a way of finding things out. An intuition."

"I wouldn't characterize it that way." Kim watched two Asian students sitting together drinking coffee and laughing. Their lives seemed easy and uncomplicated. She envied them. "What about Mr. Lincoln? Could he hire a private investigator for Mike?"

"In case you don't know it, Kim, a P.I. costs a lot of money. Mike isn't exactly loaded and I don't think you are either. I know I'm not. That has to be a last resort. You've found several murderers. You've got an instinct for it."

"I'm not so certain of that," she said.

"Will you try? For Mike's sake?"

"You know I will," Kim said. "Have you got any leads?"

Bert spread her hands. "Nada."

"Well, we know a lot of background, don't we? Mike and Evelyn both attended high school here in town. So they knew people in Webster Township, some of the same people. I'll talk to Mike after work and get the names of Evelyn's friends. That's a starting point. Meantime, do you think if you apologized Captain Nash would relent and let you back on the case?"

Bert shook her head. "I don't think so. Something he said was troubling. He said that the order came from above and he'd be screwed if I wasn't off the case."

"Who's up above?"

"It would be Chief Morgan," Bert said. "He's got the juice."

Kim stiffened. "I should make an appointment to talk to him, as a concerned citizen."

"Careful. You've been kept out of it so far. Mess with him and he might go after you for conspiracy to commit murder."

Kim raised her chin. "I'm not afraid of him."

"You should be. He's got a reign of terror going in the community. When Mayor Ryan tried to get rid of him, the chief had his car ticketed everywhere he went. When that bit of intimidation didn't work, he had the mayor's car blown up in the civic center parking lot. He's slick. No one could prove the chief was responsible, but everybody knew he was behind it. Ryan's going to be a one-term mayor. He won't run again. He's too scared. Watch your back with Chief Morgan."

"I suppose he believes himself to be above the law," Kim said.

"Hell, girl, he is the law! And no one dares cross him."

"You do want me play detective though, don't you? Well, I have to talk to him. But I will be polite." That was an easy promise to keep. It wasn't in her to be rude to anyone.

"Just be careful."

"Very careful," Kim agreed.

Chapter Twenty-Seven

Kim was distracted for the rest of the morning, thinking about what Bert had told her. On her lunch break, she used her cell and phoned Webster Township police headquarters. By nature a shy woman, Kim made few telephone calls with the exception of her mother who she phoned once a week on Sunday mornings. But this call was absolutely necessary.

When Kim told the dispatcher that she needed to talk to Chief Morgan, she found herself holding the phone for quite some time. Finally she was told that the chief could not be reached at this time.

"I must see him as soon as possible," Kim said. "This is Kim Reynolds. It concerns the Gardner murder investigation. The matter is urgent." That at least would get the attention of the woman at the other end of the telephone.

"If you hold, I can put you through to one of our detectives."

Kim swallowed hard. "No, I will only talk to Chief Morgan in person."

"The chief will be in tomorrow. Can you come by at 10 a.m.?"

Kim checked her schedule. She would be working later hours. "That will be fine."

When she hung up the phone, Kim realized her hands were sweating and her heart was palpitating. Still, it had to be done. They said Chief Morgan was a formidable man. She would find out just how formidable tomorrow morning.

Kim distrusted the police in general. Chief Morgan sounded like just the sort of law enforcement official she most wanted to avoid. Unlike Bert, Kim was reluctant to confront people. She never discussed religion or politics, avoiding argument in any form whenever possible. In truth, Kim had little respect for those in positions of authority. She didn't automatically trust their integrity.

But she would have to talk with the police chief if she were to help Mike. If he knew what she intended, Mike would have insisted she not get further involved. But Mike needed her help. That was what mattered.

She decided to do some research on Morgan. Who was this man who ruled a large New Jersey township with an iron fist? She remained at the library after her shift ended and started digging.

Sam Morgan it seemed was descended from a family that had been land granted in the Colonial era. The Morgans were reportedly related to the famous pirate, Captain Henry Morgan. They were supporters of the American cause during the Revolutionary War, and family members had served in the Continental Army. The family had prestige, money and power. The information did nothing to bolster Kim's confidence in dealing with the man.

"So exactly what did you want to tell me about the Gardner case?" Morgan said.

Kim licked her dry lips. She hadn't bothered to remove her wool coat. She shifted in the uncomfortable wooden chair.

"Lieutenant Gardner could not, would not, murder his wife."

Morgan leaned back in his chair and smiled, the kind of superior smile a teacher might bestow on a mentally challenged student. "You wouldn't be just a little prejudiced?"

"Not really. I admit I care a great deal about Lieutenant Gardner. But I know him to be a decent, honorable man. You seem to be a shrewd judge of character. Won't you use some of your influence to have this case investigated further?"

Morgan bridged his fingers and stared at her for a long moment. "I won't interfere. It would be inappropriate. I don't want it to appear that I lack confidence in the abilities of my detectives."

The man had sharp features, certainly in no way handsome, but there was a hard intelligence clicking away behind the phony, paternal façade.

"I wouldn't expect you to interfere. However, would it be possible for Detective St. Croix to do some further investigation?"

"Why would I do that when Detective Mitchell is doing a thorough job? No, I will not interfere unless there's a serious breach. I think you should be taking this up with Captain Nash, not me." He stood up indicating that the interview was at an end.

Eager as she was to escape, Kim could not let it end like this. "Chief, everyone knows you're a powerful man in this community. It's natural that I would come to you for help." Maybe flattery would help. According to Shakespeare, Caesar was caught by flattery. She was feeling pretty desperate.

"Just what do you think I can do?"

"Lieutenant Gardner is your best detective. I'm certain you wouldn't want to lose him. I'm only asking that you allow Detective St. Croix to look into Evelyn Gardner's homicide a bit further."

"I'll think about it," he said. "But I'm promising you nothing. St. Croix is an angry young person. She's unpredictable. She doesn't always think or behave logically."

"Bert cares about people and about justice."

"Maybe too much." He went on, "Let me tell you something. Anyone is capable of murder if pushed too far, even Lieutenant Gardner. He had Marine training. He also had means, motive and opportunity. Those are facts, and they weigh more heavily than your emotional attachment."

She left the chief's office and walked out of police headquarters into the civic square. The day had lost its early promise of sunlight. The trees were barren and bent to a freezing wind. Kim pulled up her coat collar and hurried to the parking lot. She had the feeling her visit had accomplished nothing.

Chapter Twenty-Eight

Kim phoned Mike as soon as she was able to take a break at work. She was relieved to find that he was at his brother's house.

She asked, "Did Bert tell you what happened?"

"Yeah, she phoned me yesterday. She thinks they're going to try and hang this guy Jameson's murder on me as well." To anyone else he would have sounded calm, but Kim could hear the tension in Mike's voice.

"I talked to Chief Morgan this morning."

"You shouldn't have done that. Mistake having anything to do with him."

"I had to try. I'm sure he's behind Bert's being reassigned. The question is why?"

"He's slick. He knows he's the man in charge. You won't get any answers from him."

"He needed someone to put the matter to him."

"I don't like it, sweetheart. I want to protect you, shelter you from harm, and here you are sticking your lovely swan's neck out for my sake."

"It's like you said, we're connected."

"Promise me you won't do anything like that again, no matter what happens."

"No promises," she said. "Mike, we need to know more about Evelyn, the people she knew in the past, especially those still in town. You knew her friends?"

"Most of them."

"Do you have any old school yearbooks?"

"That stuff's in the basement at the house."

"Why don't I meet you at your house after I get off work this evening? It'll be late, but . . ."

"I'll drive down and start searching for Evelyn's old yearbooks before you arrive."

"Sounds good."

"One other thing, Kim, I just want you to know no matter what happens, I love you and I always will."

Kim's breath caught. "I love you too. We're going to figure this out." She prayed it was true.

Walking back into Mike's house again wasn't easy. Coming here before, she had been with Bert, and that had been reassuring. Tonight, in the darkness a sensation of *otherness* attacked her. There was a residue of evil. She had the strange thought that if anyone were ever to live in this house again, it would have to be exorcized of bad vibes. She didn't sense Evelyn's spirit haunting the place. But Kim knew she could never live in a house where someone had died violently.

The front door was not locked. It reminded her of the night she had found Evelyn's body. As she looked into the living room and saw the chalk marks and blood stains on the carpet, Mike spoke from the darkness.

"She's not here," he said, and flipped on the lights.

"I know, but murder leaves an impression."

Mike took her hands. As if he had read her mind, he said, "Evelyn may have destroyed our enjoyment and love of the house but not our relationship. I will sell, abandon or bulldoze this house. But I promise you, my family will never live here again. You have my word. It's going to take time but we'll build ourselves a new home and a new life. Do you believe me?"

"I do. I have faith in you." She looked into his eyes and felt the connection between them growing strong than ever.

Mike kissed her. His warmth seeped into her.

"Where are those old yearbooks? I think we should go through them and see if there are any clues."

"Maybe they'll jog something loose in my noggin." Mike led her into the kitchen.

Kim had always liked this room. In the daytime it was sunny and cheerful and looked out on the sloping woodlands and stream behind the house. Beyond the stream there was more forest, designated as Green Acres land where no one was allowed to build. She loved it best in the summer. Tonight, snow had started to fall lightening the dark sky.

She sat down at the kitchen table where Mike had placed two yearbooks and a dusty cardboard box. Mike sat next to her.

"One yearbook represents my senior year and the other was Evelyn's. She was a year behind me."

"I'd like to look at yours first," Kim said. She wiped away some of the dust that had collected on the yearbook.

"Don't think anyone's looked at this stuff for years," he said.

Kim began flipping through the pages for any familiar faces: Evelyn, Mike, or anyone else she might know. She stopped here and there examining names, activities, class groups, sports and academics. Mike looked so young and handsome in his varsity football uniform. He'd also been first baseman on the baseball team.

"Quite the athlete," she said looking up at him.

He shrugged. "Just a typical jock. Any excuse not to study too hard."

"A very studly jock," she said with a teasing smile.

"Glad you think so." He leaned over and kissed the tip of her nose. "I'd like to see pictures of you as a kid."

She shuddered. "I don't want to go back there."

"Bet you were sexy and cute."

"Mike, only you think I'm sexy."

He turned his head to one side. "Yeah, right. That school principal Anderson wanted you bad, probably still does, and what about that English professor? Those guys think you're super hot just like I do."

Kim laughed. "They may like me but it's not because I'm sexy."

"Guess again. Good reference librarians are what turn guys on."

"Really? And here I thought it was blondes wearing tight

dresses and lots of make-up." She didn't mention Evelyn's name. She didn't have to.

"Maybe for some. Mature guys know better. Me, I like a woman with character who doesn't need a lot of make-up to be beautiful. Your radiance shines from within." Mike kissed her again and Kim found herself responding.

She sat back breathless. "You are distracting me from the business at hand."

"Kissing you is a lot more fun than rummaging through moldy mementos."

"We need to do it though."

He let out a sigh. "Guess we do at that. Though I'm not so certain we'll find anything useful. It was another lifetime, a much less complicated one."

They resumed looking through Mike's old yearbook. He was right. There was nothing there that could be considered valuable. A much younger and prettier Evelyn showed up as part of the cheerleading squad. Kim glanced at pictures of the other girls as well. How innocent and hopeful they all looked, the world full of infinite possibilities.

Evelyn's yearbook had a number of pictures that interested Kim. "I see Evelyn was co-captain of the cheerleading squad her senior year."

Mike looked over at the photo. "I'd forgotten about that. Let's see, the other girl was Laura Berg. She was Evelyn's rival in popularity. As I recall they both wanted to be Homecoming Queen. Evelyn won." Mike flipped the pages. "Yeah, there she is."

Kim studied the photo. Evelyn was on the arm of a smiling teenage boy. The face looked somewhat familiar. She glanced at the name. "Thomas Ryan — Mayor Ryan?"

"One in the same. He was always popular too, a politician even at that age. He reigned as Homecoming King."

Kim was pensive. "Mike, you said Evelyn was your high school sweetheart."

He looked over at her. "She was, but I joined the Marines after graduating high school. I couldn't expect Evelyn to just sit at home while I was gone."

"So she did date other boys?"

"Well, we didn't really talk about it. But sure, she must have."

"What about Mayor Ryan?"

"Couldn't have been anything much there. Thomas Ryan married Laura Berg."

"Evelyn's rival? That's interesting."

"What are you thinking?"

Kim shook her head. "Only that it's an intriguing bit of information."

They looked through the yearbook some more. There was Evelyn cheering the football team on to victory. But nothing else really stood out.

"What's in that cardboard box?" Kim asked.

"Some of Evelyn's old stuff. When she left me, she took very little with her. Just folded her tent and took off so to speak. I never had the heart to throw any of her old stuff away. Guess I thought she might someday come back and want it, or maybe the girls would want to go through it eventually."

Kim reached inside the box, which smelled faintly of mold.

There were cards, photos, even letters from Mike that he'd written when he was overseas.

Kim could see the sadness in Mike's eyes as he glanced at the memorabilia.

"You don't have to look at this. I can do it by myself," Kim said. "I do a lot of searching for information at work. It's what I do best."

"I disagree. There are things you do even better. I can testify to that." His eyes twinkled as he teased her. He brought a large callused hand over her smaller one. "You don't need to spare me. We'll look at this together."

Kim peered inside the carton again and brought out what looked like a girl's diary. "Evelyn's?"

Mike gave a small nod. "She used to write in a diary when she was young. I remember her telling me she kept it locked so her mother and sister couldn't read it."

"Are her parents alive?" Kim asked.

"Just her father. After her mother died, it was pretty much just her and her dad. Evelyn had a sister, Maryann, but she was older and they were never close. Maryann left home after their mother died. After she and I were married, Evelyn's dad retired from his job and moved to Texas, which was just as well."

"Why do you say that?"

"I never liked the guy. Something about him made me uncomfortable, as if he wasn't quite right. I can't explain it exactly. Just a feeling I had about him."

"I can understand that. Certain people send off bad auras." Kim attempted to open the diary but the lock held.

"Allow me," Mike said. He got up, went to his utility drawer, moved items around and then came up with a small tool that looked to Kim like a lock pick. With one twist, he had the lock open and handed the diary back to her.

"I guess you could always become a burglar if you can't get your detective job back."

"I have many talents." He gave her an insinuating smile.

"I won't bother to reply to that. I might forget about our purpose in being here."

Kim opened the diary. As she did, several photos dropped out and fell on the table.

Kim studied the first photo, which had been taken at a dance. It showed a young Mike looking awkward in a tuxedo while Evelyn beamed into the camera, dressed in evening gown and corsage, blond hair piled high on her head.

"My senior prom," Mike said. "I hated going, but Evelyn was looking forward to it and insisted."

Kim studied the second photo. There was Evelyn again smiling at the photographer. She looked older and more sophisticated. The young boy with her wasn't Mike but Kim thought she recognized Evelyn's date. "Evelyn's senior prom," she surmised.

"Right."

"Her date was Drew Mitchell?"

Mike shrugged. "Guess so. I wasn't around. She wasn't going to miss out. We didn't discuss it."

"It certainly looks like Detective Mitchell in the photo. So you weren't the jealous type in those days?"

Mike frowned, his lips tightening. "Evelyn made me feel guilty about not being there for her."

"I see," Kim said in a dry voice. "I thought that Detective Mitchell was younger than Evelyn for some reason."

"Evelyn just gave the impression of being older."

"So Evelyn dated him?"

Mike looked down. "I suppose she did. We never really talked about it. It could have just been a prom thing. I wasn't jealous. Mitch was kind of an immature kid. She needed someone to take her and he was available. No big thing."

"What do you know about Drew Mitchell as a person?"

"Not much, really. We've never been friendly. He's a closed, private sort of guy."

"Is he married?"

Mike reflected. "He's never mentioned a wife."

"Girlfriend?"

Mike shook his head. "Never talks about one."

Kim found that interesting. Usually when people worked together they spoke of family or friends. Why was Drew Mitchell so guarded? She wanted to know more about the detective.

"Would you object if I took Evelyn's diary with me? I want to take my time reading it."

"Feel free."

"Good. And I want to take a few of her publicity photos as well."

Mike placed his hand on hers. "Sweetheart, please be careful about asking questions. Get Bert to help you. There's a murderer running around, and you might provoke him to act again. I don't want you to risk your life."

"I'll be careful. And I promise I'll let you know if I find anything of interest."

Mike looked at his watch. "Getting late. What time do you go in tomorrow?"

"I'm off. It works out well. I have the late shift on Saturday. I won't be getting home until around midnight. So I get a weekday to make up for it."

Mike scowled. "That parking deck at the university isn't safe. I don't like you walking out there late at night by yourself."

"It's part of the job."

"Call me an hour before you get off. I'll meet you, escort you to your car and follow you home."

She hugged him. "Thank you, Mr. Knight-in-Shining-Armor, but that's not necessary. I keep pepper spray in my handbag."

"Yeah, all well and good. Look, I know I'm old-fashioned but humor me, okay? There was a woman abducted and raped from that parking deck, and a guy was slashed and robbed another time."

"I could request an escort from the school," she conceded. "The university provides them when possible." She wasn't likely to do so though, since she disliked asking for favors.

"I'll phone you on Saturday," Mike said.

"Okay, I will now sing a chorus of *Someone to Watch Over Me*."

"Nothing like the oldies," he said. "But it's not a joking matter."

"I never thought it was."

"Let's get out of here. I'll follow you back to your apartment."

"You don't have to do that," she said. "You ought to be home with the girls."

"I'm with them a lot. Besides, they're going to sleep about now. I kind of thought we could spend some quality time together not talking about Evelyn's murder." He gave her a slow, sexy smile.

"What do you have in mind?"

Mike took her into his arms. "Ms. Reynolds, I'd rather show you than tell you."

Chapter Twenty-Nine

Mike Gardner was in a good mood when he returned to his brother's house the following afternoon. It had been great spending time alone with Kim. He dreamed of them being married, sleeping together every night, making love often with nothing coming between them. That was his idea of heaven.

No one was home at Chuck's house. As soon as he dropped his keys and wallet on an end table, the phone began ringing. He picked it up, noting the caller I.D.

"Gardner here."

Captain Nash sounded grim. "Mike, I need you to come into headquarters right now."

"What's up?"

"Talk about it when you get here." The captain hung up.

A voice in the back of Gardner's head said: *Don't go.* But if he didn't show, they'd get an arrest warrant out for him. He wasn't a criminal. No way would he act like one.

Kim was having a strange dream. Mike was calling to her. It was a warning of some sort. But she couldn't understand him.

"I can't hear you. What are you saying?"

His words were vague, unclear. Why couldn't she see him better? Why was he so insubstantial?

She reached out to Mike and he was gone. A noise kept repeating. Kim's eyes fluttered open and she realized that a doorbell was ringing. Her doorbell. She roused herself from the lethargy she was feeling.

"Who is it?" she called out.

"Bert. Hurry up. I feel like I've been ringing your doorbell forever and it's freezing out here."

Kim hurried to open the door. "Sorry, I was asleep."

"At four in the afternoon?"

"I was tired. I kind of conked out." She wasn't about to tell Bert that Mike had made love to her for a good part of the night, worn her out in a good way.

"They've taken Mike back into custody, returned him to jail. He wanted me to tell you."

Kim fell back on the sofa bed. She felt as if she'd been punched in the chest. "God, no."

Bert paced back and forth across the small space. "They're blaming him for Jameson's death. Bail's been revoked."

"I'll call the lawyer."

"I don't think he'll be much help."

"Why would you say that? He might be."

Bert looked frustrated. "You're right. Call him."

"There's something else. Mike and I made a couple of interesting discoveries last evening." As she went into the small kitchen to prepare coffee, she explained, "First, Drew Mitchell and Evelyn were well acquainted. He was her date for her senior prom. He never let on that he so much as knew her. Now why would that be? Bert, what do you know about Mitchell's personal life?"

"Nothing at all. He's close-mouthed, and anyway he hates me. Accused me of being a lesbian."

"He actually said that?"

"Pretty much. Claims he was hitting on April and she spurned his advances. Knowing we're friends, he blamed me. Thinks of me as a rival. Frankly, I think the guy's a bigoted creep."

"I get similar vibes."

"Figure there was something between him and Evelyn? Maybe something he wouldn't have wanted Mike to know about?"

Kim placed cookies on a gold patterned plate. "Could be. I'm just not certain."

"I got an idea. Let's head over to the Galaxy. April's

working this evening. We can talk to her about it. Three heads together."

"Good idea. The other thing was, Evelyn and Mayor Ryan apparently dated at one time."

"Our Mayor Ryan?" Bert seemed astonished.

"After Mike left for the service."

"That girl got around, didn't she?" Bert said.

Bert drove them to the Galaxy Lounge. The bar was quiet, for which Kim was grateful. They took a table at the rear. April Nevins arrived to take their drink order. The Galaxy Lounge, where April worked as a cocktail waitress, was a relatively new establishment in Webster Township. The locals rarely went there, too new and fancy for their tastes. But it drew business among the emigrant New Yorkers who occupied the luxury condos and garden apartments in the township.

"So what would you like to order?" April asked with a warm smile.

April's blond highlighted hair was pulled back from her face and neatly parted down the middle. Her costume was anything but prim. A black velvet micro skirt barely brushed the tops of her thighs. Her white satin blouse, cut very low, loosely covered her breasts. Male customers would have to be made of stone not to notice.

"Tomato juice for me," Bert said.

"I'll have a cranberry juice," Kim said.

"How about a glass of wine? You like merlot, don't you? Kick back and relax," April said.

Kim nodded and let April change the order. She wasn't much for alcohol, but she also wasn't in the mood to argue about anything this evening. She felt tense and exhausted. The thought of Mike back in jail stressed her.

Kim glanced around the lounge. It was dark, the walls black and tablecloths blood red. Tapered red candles burned at each table.

Soft music was being piped in from somewhere. The only unusual thing was the ceiling: where some aspiring Michelangelo had painted the universe. Kim thought about the last time she'd been here . . .

Mike had brought her.

He'd raised his glass. "I want to offer a toast to the woman I love." He'd taken a sip of his beer, said, "I have something for you," and reached into his jacket pocket. The small black velvet box he handed her held a diamond ring.

Kim viewed it through a mist of tears.

"If it's not what you want, we can return it and you can pick out something else. I know it has to be sized too. I wasn't certain of the fit."

"It's beautiful."

"The jeweler said it's a perfect blue-white stone. I don't know much about jewelry, but I thought you'd like it."

"I do, very much."

"So can we make it official? Will you marry me?"

She'd swallowed hard. There would never be a man more perfect for her than Mike Gardner. They were so right for each other. He loved her and she loved him.

"Yes, Mike. I'll marry you."

His smile was as bright as the diamond.

"Kim? What's going on? You've got a weird expression on your face," Bert said.

Kim blinked. "Sorry. I was just remembering. Mike brought me here the night he proposed."

April brought their drinks and a bowl of mixed nuts. She lingered. "You're both looking kind of down. What's wrong?"

"Mike Gardner's back in jail," Bert said.

"That sucks! Hold on, I'll be right back." She walked over to the bar, said, "I'm taking my break now."

The bald-headed bartender glared at April. "You're not supposed to break until Angel shows up. You know that."

"Look around, Frank. It's slow. Besides, my friends need me. So don't give me grief." April turned on her stacked heels and came back to the table. She sat opposite Bert. "So why did they take him in again? I thought he was out on bail."

"He was, but now they think he killed this other guy, a pal of Evelyn's." Bert stared down at her drink.

April turned to Kim. "I'm real sorry. I wish I could help."

"Don't we all," Bert said.

Kim said, "I took some pictures of Evelyn from the house. We don't know what she did with her days since she returned to town. I was thinking of taking the pictures around to see if anyone knew her recent whereabouts."

"Kind of a long shot," Bert said.

"I suppose it is. Just an idea."

"Stop being so defeatist. Show me the pictures," April said. "I know the regulars. If she came in with any one of them, I might remember."

Kim pulled out two of the glossies from her handbag. April took them and stared.

"What do you think?" Kim asked.

April said, "You know I *have* seen her before."

Chapter Thirty

"*Are you certain* Evelyn Gardner came in here?" Bert said.

"I'm sure. Honor bright. I'm not making it up." April twirled a strand of hair.

Bert exchanged an excited look with Kim, and then leaned forward. "Was she with anyone?"

April gave a quick nod.

"Anyone you recognize?"

"There were two times that I can remember. Once she was with Mayor Ryan. I recognized him because his face is in the newspaper. I've seen him here with his wife a few times too. That's why I took a look at the woman he was talking to."

"Did they look romantic? You know like holding hands?" Bert asked.

"No. I kind of remember they looked like they were arguing. I wasn't their server though. So I didn't catch any of the conversation."

"You mentioned a second time?" Bert prodded.

"Oh, yeah. She was with some older dude. He chose a back booth, very private. I did serve them and I recognized her. He kept his voice low and neither of them talked in my presence. Seemed like an intense conversation."

"Would you recognize that man again?" Bert asked.

"Maybe. He had a kind of air of authority about him. Like he thought he was someone important, a big shot. That was my impression anyway. He left an average size tip though. So I didn't check him out too carefully. I always take special notice of big tippers. That way if they come in again and I catch their table, I provide super good service."

"April, you know Detective Mitchell, don't you?" Kim asked.

April snorted with derision. "He's a real sleaze. Comes in here once in a while, always tries to hit on me or Angel."

"Was he ever here with Evelyn?" Kim asked.

April shook her head. "Not that I know of. Then again, I'm not here all the time."

"Anything else you can remember?" Bert asked.

"Not really. Sorry."

"Think about it some more. I'll be in touch."

"Sure. I want to help any way I can. Frank's giving me the evil eye. Gotta get going." April looked down at Bert's glass of tomato juice. "You should drink that before it clots." Then she was off. Two businessmen were waiting to be seated.

"Here's irony for you," Bert said. "Mayor Ryan's funeral home's where Evelyn's laid out."

"I'll drop by and pay my respects," Kim said.

"And maybe chat Ryan?"

"Absolutely. And his wife as well. Mike and I found that Mrs. Ryan knew Evelyn well back in the day. They were rivals in high school."

"Want me to come with you?"

"They might say more if it's not an official police visit. Besides, with Mayor Ryan and Chief Morgan mortal enemies, he's not going to trust a township detective."

"Okay, but if you need help, call me, day or night." Bert's cell phone sounded. She took it from her pocket, saw the caller I.D. and sighed.

"St. Croix," she said. Then she listened. "Be right there." She flipped the phone shut. "They're wondering where I am. Got to get back to headquarters."

Ryan's Funeral Home was out on the highway, set back with trees and shrubbery in front. A large parking lot wrapped around the sides and the back. The lot was almost empty.

Kim hated funeral homes and cemeteries. The last funeral she'd attended had been for her friend Lorette Campbell, and there she had heard the voices of the dead as well as the living. It had been pure torture. Kim trembled at the memory.

"Where would I find Mr. Ryan?" she asked the young woman who was taking coats.

"He's in with the bereaved," the young woman answered. "Will you need tissues?"

"No thanks."

The young woman looked surprised. Kim found the main viewing room without any difficulty and was relieved to see that the casket was closed. White lilies adorned it. There were few people present. She didn't see the funeral director at first. The room was dimly lit and her eyes needed a moment to adjust. She heard Ryan before she saw him.

"What are you doing here?" The funeral director's voice was an accusatory hiss, not what one expected from a man in his line of work. Kim turned and realized the question had not been directed to her.

"I knew the deceased." Kim recognized the voice of the second man.

"I think you're just here to cause trouble," Mayor Ryan said.

Chief Morgan chuckled. "Are you really that stupid or are you tripping over your immense ego?"

The mayor and the police chief faced each at the back of the room. Ryan was tall with a florid complexion. From his yearbook picture, Kim knew he had been handsome as a teenager. Now he looked as if he'd eaten desserts at too many fund-raising dinners and avoided exercise. In contrast, there was nothing flabby about Chief Morgan, although he was much older than the mayor and a head shorter. Morgan had an olive complexion, a hawkish nose, a pit bull jaw, and small but shrewd eyes that seemed to miss nothing. For a moment, his gaze flickered in her direction and Kim had a sense of foreboding. This man could be dangerous and a bad enemy.

A woman came up and took Ryan by the hand. "We need you in the other room," she said.

Then she turned to Chief Morgan. "So good that you could come today. Please excuse us."

The woman was certainly smooth. Kim recognized Laura Berg Ryan from her high school picture. She was holding up better than her husband. Although her waistline had thickened, Mrs. Ryan was not unattractive.

Kim followed them from the viewing room, turning only once to look back, and noticed that Chief Morgan's steady gaze was focused on her. She did not like the expression in his eyes.

Kim watched as Mrs. Ryan organized prayer books, then slipped in beside her.

"Not many people here for Evelyn Gardner," Kim said in a neutral voice.

"There wouldn't be, would there?"

"I don't know. Wasn't she popular in town when she went to high school?"

Laura Ryan let out an unladylike snort. "Yeah, right." Then she cocked a dark brow. "You weren't in my high school class. You're too young. How do you know about Evelyn?"

Laura Ryan was no fool. And Kim wasn't a good liar. There was no choice but to tell the truth. "I'm a friend of Lieutenant Gardner," she said.

"You're the one the newspaper article mentioned, aren't you?" Her eyes narrowed. "Evelyn came back to town and wrecked things for you and him. Yeah, that was Evelyn, all right. She always wanted guys if they belonged to some other female. Very competitive. She went after my Thomas when we were seniors in high school. She was such a jealous cat. She'd had Mike Gardner, the best athlete in school, but he got away from her for a while by joining the service. So then she tried to snatch my Tommy. I didn't let her get away with it though."

"How could you stop her?"

Laura Ryan gave a nasty laugh. "I told her I'd kill her."

Kim stared at the woman. There was an almost maniacal gleam in her eyes.

"But of course you didn't mean it," Kim said.

"Didn't I? Well, it really didn't matter much anyway. Tommy assured me he had no interest in her. And after that Evelyn started seeing Drew Mitchell, even went to the prom with him."

"So they had a relationship?"

Laura shrugged. "Who can say? Tell you one thing, I wouldn't blame Mike Gardner for killing that one. She was as rotten and selfish as they come."

"She wanted to be an actress," Kim said. "Maybe that goes hand and hand with a big ego."

"Well, she fooled a lot of people for a while, most of them male, but she never fooled me. I always knew the kind of person she was."

With that, Laura excused herself. Kim went back to the viewing room. As funeral director, Tom Ryan was in full sympathy mode. He shook hands and expressed condolences to anyone who happened to walk in. Kim could easily see him wooing voters. He could have had his own acting career.

Kim waited until there were no more people for him to greet and then she went over and allowed him to shake her hand. His hand felt unpleasantly damp.

"Mayor Ryan, I understand you knew Evelyn Gardner personally."

He pulled at his collar. "I didn't know her that well. She was in high school with me, but after that I didn't see much of her. We moved in different circles." He glanced around.

"Is being a mortician a family thing?" she asked trying to keep him from walking away.

"Ryan's Funeral Parlor has been in town for three generations. Long before they built all the newer housing complexes."

She dredged up a bit of her local lore. "And Rourke's was your competition?" she asked.

The mayor turned his head in surprise. "Well, not exactly. There was plenty of work for both of us."

"I suppose you can always depend on people dying."

"It's a real solid business all right. The Rourkes and the Ryans did okay. But Rourke made one big mistake."

"What was that?" Kim asked.

"The senior citizens needed a meeting place. They were planning a health festival. Mr. Rourke heard about it, and he was a big benefactor in town. He donated the space as a courtesy. But McKenna, president of the local senior group, claimed the old folks balked when they heard about it. He said it was bad for the morale of their group to hold a senior citizen health festival in a funeral parlor. Even told the local news reporter that Rourke was insensitive to the feelings of seniors. And Rourke was getting up in years himself. He was deeply offended. Anyway, he sold out to me and decided to retire. So now I got double the operation."

"Congratulations. It's a wonder that you have time to serve the community as mayor."

He leaned closer. "I doubt I'll run for another term. Chief Morgan's making life difficult for us. My wife's urging me to ease up. My father died of a heart attack when he wasn't much older than me. I want to live to enjoy my success."

"I understand." Her tone was sympathetic. Kim's maternal grandparents had both died early of heart disease.

"Say, you're a good listener. Maybe you'd like to meet me for a drink one evening?"

She tensed. "You mean like you met Evelyn Gardner?"

His face reddened. "Her? What gave you that idea? Haven't seen her since high school. Not until now that is. Terrible thing about her husband murdering her."

"Isn't it?" Kim said.

Laura Ryan joined them and took her husband's arm in a possessive gesture. "Darling, you're needed." She gave Kim a hostile look.

Kim retrieved her coat and made for the door.

She had learned a couple of things. Laura Ryan was a jealous, possessive wife. And Thomas Ryan was a womanizer. Beyond that, he'd lied about not having seen Evelyn recently. April placed them at the Galaxy. After that, she had only guesswork. Evelyn *might* have had an affair with Ryan. Wanting money, Evelyn *might* have tried to blackmail Ryan. Either the mayor or his wife could have had a motive for killing Evelyn.

As Kim walked to her car in the dark parking lot, she had the uncomfortable sensation that someone was watching her. She whirled around but saw no one. Still the feeling persisted. Hurrying, she unlocked her car door. Her hands trembled. As she drove away from the funeral parlor, Kim glanced in her rear view mirror. When she saw no lights, she sighed. Maybe she was just imagining things—or not.

Laura watched the attractive younger woman walk away. She turned to her husband. "Tom, stay away from her."

Tom Ryan colored. "Honey, I have no interest in anyone but you. It hurts me that you would think otherwise."

"That, my darling husband, is so much crap. I'm just warning you for your own good. That particular woman represents trouble. I'm an excellent judge of character. Listen to me."

Tom looked at her. "I admit I do flirt a bit, but it's harmless."

"Like with Evelyn Gardner?" Laura nodded toward the casket at the end of the room.

The funeral director exchanged a meaningful look with his wife. "I don't think we should talk about her ever again."

"I hope that's possible," Laura said. She ground down on her lower molars. She loved her husband, but that did not alter the fact she realized he could behave in a foolish manner at times. And when that happened, it was up to her to fix things.

Chapter Thirty-One

"It's not looking good," Lincoln said to Gardner. "They're planning to go after you for the two homicides."

"Yeah, I got that. Tell me something I don't already know." Gardner usually took things in stride, but he was feeling down. Being stuck in this cage was getting to him. He realized that solitary confinement was for his own safety, but it wasn't easy to endure. There were no windows, just gray cinderblock walls. Meals were slid through a slot. The trays were returned the same way.

The worst part was he couldn't see his family or Kim. Bert would probably be allowed in at some point since she was a police detective, but for the time being, his lawyer was Gardner's only connection with the outside world.

He sat across from his lawyer at a table. At least that amenity had been allowed.

"I'm trying to get us a preliminary hearing."

"Would that help?"

"I think so. Here's how it works. The state puts on evidence to show the court why the matter should be set for trial, and the defense attorney has the ability to cross-examine witnesses. Some prosecutors would rather avoid a preliminary hearing because they don't want to expose their witnesses at that early a stage and elect to go to the Grand Jury instead. Grand Jury proceedings are secret, and defense lawyers can only be present if and when their own client testifies."

"So it's not likely the D.A.'s office will go for a preliminary hearing."

"Maybe not," Lincoln conceded, "but it's still worth a try."

"What if my case goes to the Grand Jury?"

Lincoln faced him with a direct gaze. "You want it straight?"

"Always."

"A prosecutor usually has no problem in getting an indictment because the Grand Jury generally only hears one side, the side of the prosecution. There's no judge to rule on the admissibility of evidence or defense lawyer to cross-examine the witnesses, and normally they hear nothing from the defense."

Gardner processed the information in as stoic a manner as he could manage. "Suppose I want to testify? Am I allowed?"

"If we decide it's in your best interest for you to testify and/or present witnesses, I can arrange for it. I would have to notify the prosecutor before the Grand Jury presentation is completed. You, personally, have a right to testify before the Grand Jury, but I would have to get permission to present other witnesses. If you do testify, I can be there with you, but I can't ask questions or make objections or be present when any witnesses you have testify."

"So we could be done with it right there and then?" Gardner felt a slight surge of hope.

"If things go well for you, the Grand Jury will not return an indictment and your case will be over, saving you a lot of hassle and money."

"Sounds good."

"We'll have to see," Lincoln said. His tone was cautious. "I won't lie to you. It's going to be an uphill battle for us all the way."

Gardner gave a quick nod. "I want this over with as soon as possible. My family is suffering."

His attorney leaned forward, lowering his voice. "You remember Juan Romerez, the accountant accused of embezzlement?"

"Of course. How's he doing?"

"Still here. Some problem with him as a flight risk. His family's down in the Dominican Republic. I couldn't get the judge to release him."

"Too bad. I have a hunch he really is innocent."

Lincoln's face didn't change expression. "I'm cynical. Seen too many criminals claim their innocence, swear it on their mother's life.

But don't worry, I'll do a good job for Romerez too. The thing is I spoke to him just before I came to see you." Lincoln glanced around, then spoke softly. "He says he overheard something. He thought it might be about you, that someone was paid off to kill you here at the jail."

"If that ape Williams was paid, they used an idiot the first time."

"It sounded as though the guards were just a little too slow," Lincoln said. "Keep that in mind, too. Watch your back." Lincoln got to his feet. "I'll be meeting with your cop friend. If she's got any leads, I'll let you know."

When Mike Gardner returned to his cell, he sized up his chances. The Marine Corps had toughened him and provided him with self-discipline. He worked out every day after leaving the service. He kept a treadmill in his basement so he could jog even in bad weather and a bench press so he could lift weights. He was still lean, well-muscled and had quick reflexes. But he wished he had a weapon handy. He got down, did a set of fifty push-ups, and felt better for the effort. The worst thing from his point of view was the sense of feeling powerless to help himself and protect his family and Kim.

Bert strode into the humanities library carrying Evie's laptop and feeling out of place. Relief swept over her when she spied Kim helping a student. She waited in silence until Kim finished working with the girl.

When Bert approached, Kim spoke as if she was just another library patron. "How can I help you?"

"Would you believe the techs haven't even looked at this computer?" Bert snapped. "I told them it was a priority. I was so angry I just snatched it back. Now I'm not sure what to do. You any good with computers?"

"Fair," Kim said. "You got Evie's passwords. That will help. We should contact the cable company. We need Mike's info to do that. His bills will have it. He might even have the original work order. Then we'll have easy access. If Evelyn used this computer to contact people we might get lucky and find some information."

"Not so easy to talk to Mike now," Bert said. "I can talk to Fred Lincoln about setting up a visit, but that all takes time."

"Leave the computer with me," Kim said. "I'll phone Chuck and Louise and ask that one of them bring Evie and the house keys to Mike's place this evening. I'll search Mike's desk for the cable bills and records. Then we can try to get the cable company to help us."

"Okay, let me know the time and I'll meet you. Right now I guess I better get back to work. There's a burglary I'm supposed to be investigating."

Kim nodded. "We're going to crack this. We know that Mayor Ryan, his wife and Detective Mitchell all had connections with Evelyn. I have Evelyn's diary. Maybe I'll find something in that."

Students were lining up at the information desk and Kim hurried to provide help.

Kim and Evie had already set up Evie's laptop by the time Bert arrived at Mike Gardner's house that evening.

"Where are your aunt and uncle?" Bert asked Evie.

"Kim told my uncle she'd bring me home later. Aunt Louise didn't come. She didn't think Jean or my cousins should come to the house on account of . . ." Evie's voice trailed off and her eyes cast downward.

Kim said, "Bert, you're going to have to place the call to the cable company. I tried but they said I wasn't the party who the bills are issued to and therefore they couldn't give me any information. They might give different answers to a police officer."

"I'll do my best."

Kim handed her the information and Bert phoned the cable

company. It took a half hour of going through several different people, but Bert managed to convince a supervisor that she was a policewoman on official business. The supervisor provided Bert with Evelyn's email address and password.

Bert let out a sigh of relief. "We're in business," she said after hanging up the phone. "We might have figured this out for ourselves though. The email address begins with *Evelyngardner* and the password is *moviestar*."

"That was so like my mother," Evie said. She began typing. The emails sprung up immediately. There were hundreds of them.

Evie stood up. "Guess you want to read these," the girl said.

Bert replaced Evie at the computer.

Most of it was trash—advertisements, job loops for actors, friendly chitchat and gossip.

But a few of the emails were interesting. "Look at this one," she said to Kim.

The email read: "Don't threaten me or you'll regret it."

Another read: "I'm calling your bluff. Don't try blackmailing me again or you'll be very sorry."

The senders had used screen names that made no sense. But their identities could be tracked down.

The important thing, Kim thought, was that these emails provided evidence that people besides Mike had motives for murdering Evelyn Gardner. Kim went through the rest of the emails. Nothing important. But on a saved draft was Evellyn's comment: "I need money. You have plenty. Don't threaten me. I'm not afraid of you. I'll text with details."

"Damn, I wish we had her cell phone!"

"Let's print out these emails," Kim said.

"I'll set up a meeting with the lawyer for tomorrow. I want him to see these."

"Can you do lunch?" Kim asked.

"I can swing it. You're sounding kind of Hollywood you know?"

Kim grinned. "Rubs off."

Evie said, "Will this help my dad?" She looked from Bert to Kim.
"We hope so," Kim said.
"Jeannie needs him," Evie said, a tear glistening in her eye.
"We all do," Kim said. She patted the girl's head.

Chapter Thirty-Two

Frederick Douglas Lincoln was munching on a fast food burger he'd picked up down the block from his office when Bert St. Croix arrived. "God, this place is seedy," she said.

"Best I can afford at the moment," he replied. "Of course, I could charge your friend and others more money for my services. Then I could afford an office that would impress you."

Bert said, "Never mind. You lawyers have an answer for everything."

"Not everything," he said. "I'm trying to figure out if you'll bite my head off if I ask you out for dinner."

She stared at him. "You really want to go out with me?"

"Why wouldn't I? You're hot."

She laughed.

"What's so funny?"

"I've been called a lot of things, but never hot."

"Okay, sexy then."

She folded her arms. "I don't dress sexy. I carry wherever I go. I'm taller than most men and stronger. And I don't exactly put on the charm or flirt."

"That's what makes you so hot."

"Really?"

"I like a woman who isn't afraid to be herself. Of course, you are a few skin shades lighter than me. Is my teasin' tan a turn-off for you?"

"No."

"But I'm not your type?"

She leaned toward him, so close he felt like laying a smacking kiss on her full lips.

"The thing is, Mr. Lincoln . . ."

"Call me Fred."

"Okay, Fred, the thing is, I've never been into men, black, white, purple, green."

"And why is that?" He saw the unflattering man-tailored pantsuit and thought, *If she's gay it's a damn shame.*

"It's kind of personal and I don't talk about it much. Let's just say my father left my mother when I was born. She was an island woman, hard-working, loving. My father was an African-American who had a love 'em and leave 'em mentality. He could screw a woman but took no responsibility for his action, just moving on to the next female foolish enough to fall for his line of bullshit. My mother raised me by herself, doing whatever kind of work she could get. Mostly, she hired out as a cleaning woman."

"A hard life."

"I'm not telling you this so you'll feel sorry for me. She's been dead for years now. So is my best friend who was a nurse. They were good women who deserved a whole lot better than they got out of life. The thing is I've never really trusted men, particularly men of color. I've always felt I had to be smarter, stronger and tougher than any of you."

He met her steady gaze. "We're not all like your father. I come from a good family. My parents are supportive. My folks love each other and they love their children. They're church-going people. I have a brother and two sisters. We all help each other. If I had a wife, I'd treat her with respect. I wouldn't walk away from her."

"Well, I guess you're not the bottom-dweller I think defense attorneys are."

He managed a wry smile. "Thanks for the compliment—I guess it was meant as a compliment?"

"Yeah, for me it was. I've got low expectations for men in general and criminal lawyers in particular. You'd have to prove yourself to me to have me trust you. Still want to have dinner with me sometime?"

"Haven't changed my mind," he said.

"I'm not easy," she said.

"That's obvious. But I'd consider it a privilege to earn your trust."

Their eyes met. Lincoln thought he detected interest. That was a start.

Kim had entered Frederick Lincoln's office without either of the two people present noticing.

"So what's going on?"

Bert started, seeming embarrassed. The lawyer gave Kim a beaming smile.

Bert said, "I was about to tell Mr. Lincoln what we discovered on Evie's computer."

As Kim settled into a chair, Bert went on: "Evelyn used her daughter's computer. There were a couple of email messages we thought you might find interesting. We printed them out."

Kim took the folded papers from her handbag and handed them to the lawyer. "What do you think?"

He read the messages. "Do you have any idea who might have written these?"

Kim looked to Bert who gave her a short nod. Kim cleared her throat. "There are three people who might possibly have been blackmailed by Evelyn. She dated Drew Mitchell, the investigating detective, back in high school. He's been in a big hurry to blame Evelyn's murder on Mike. I have this feeling that Evelyn knew something about the man he wouldn't want others to know. She could have been seeing him again."

"Your feeling doesn't count. But if they *were* involved, we could get Mitchell thrown off the case." The lawyer tapped his pen on his desktop. "Who else?"

"Thomas Ryan. He's both the mayor of Webster Township and the most important funeral director. I'm certain he was seeing Evelyn on the sly. We have a waitress who saw the two of them drinking together. I don't think he'd want that known. His wife's the jealous type. Evelyn could have hit him up for money." Kim observed she had the lawyer's full attention now. She cleared her throat and continued. "Then there's Laura Ryan, the mayor's wife. She seems to be a possessive woman. She and Evelyn were high school rivals for Thomas's attentions among other things."

"Sounds good, but we're going to need more."

"Wouldn't those emails be proof that Evelyn had enemies?"

"Not as good as a neighbor who saw someone other than Mike with Evelyn before she died."

"Police Chief Morgan had Bert removed from further investigation on the case. Mike told us some time ago that he's known to be corrupt. I spoke with him and got the feeling that he was hiding information. Maybe Evelyn had something on him as well."

"Nice—the mayor, the mayor's wife, the police chief and the lead detective. I'm glad you didn't come up with anything political."

Bert stood up. "Isn't this enough to establish doubt?"

"It establishes plenty of doubt. But it doesn't tell you how a jury will react. I don't mean to push you. I'd like nothing better than to go before the Grand Jury and convince them not to hand down an indictment. And this stuff, if we can make it solid, will help. The worse it looks for the powers that be, the better it will look for Mike."

Chapter Thirty-Three

The phone was ringing when Kim entered her apartment that evening. She grabbed the receiver on the second ring.

"I hope I'm not disturbing you," said Louise Gardner.

"No." Kim laid her keys and handbag on the end table. "Is there a problem?"

"I'm really sorry to bother you. It's just that Evie and Jean have been arguing. They're upset about their parents. I've tried to talk to them but they just ignore me and keep on fighting."

"Why don't I drive over and spend some time with them?"

"Could you? That would be good." Kim heard the relief in the older woman's voice.

"I'll just open a can of soup for supper and then be over in an hour or so."

"Why don't you come here for dinner? We've got plenty."

"I don't want to intrude on your family dinner."

"You wouldn't be. We'd love the company."

Louse sounded genuine.

"If you're sure I wouldn't be imposing."

"Absolutely not."

Kim changed out of her work clothes into jeans, turtleneck and hoodie. It felt good putting her feet into warm socks and comfortable sneakers.

Dinner with the Gardners was unpleasant. Chuck wasn't due home from work until later. Mark, age nine, and Jerry, twelve, started shoving each other at the table. Louise yelled at them to behave. Evie didn't talk to anyone, ate very little and excused herself before the meal was over. Jean's eyes were red-rimmed.

Louise served meatloaf, mashed potatoes and green beans with slivered almonds. For dessert, she brought out a large bowl of fresh fruit: apples, oranges, bananas and grapes. It was a substantial, nutritious meal, and Kim complimented Louise, who looked pleased that someone recognized her efforts. Kim insisted on helping with the cleanup.

"Really, the children should be helping, not you. You're a guest here." Louise's face flushed with embarrassment.

"Not a problem. I appreciate a hot meal, especially on a cold day. I'm usually too tired after work to cook for myself."

"And here I troubled you to drive all the way out here."

"I like the girls. I want to spend time with them."

Although Louise might be plain-looking, when she smiled as she was doing now she lit up.

After the cleanup, Kim went looking for Jean. She found the girl zoned out in front of the TV set in the recreation room. Nearby, Mark and Jerry were practicing karate moves on each other. Kim had the strong suspicion this would deteriorate into a fist fight.

"May I?" Kim indicated the television and Jean shrugged. Kim turned down the sound. "I thought we might talk a bit. It's been a long time."

Jean nodded. "Since Mom came home." Tears formed in Jean's eyes. "I can't believe she's dead."

Kim squeezed Jean's hand. "I know losing her again has been very hard on you."

"I miss her. I was so happy when she came home." Jean's lower lip trembled. "I hardly remembered what she looked like. It was never the same at our house after she left."

Kim placed her arm around the girl. "It's okay to cry and feel sad."

Jean sobbed. Kim patted the child's back. "It will get better."

"People are saying my dad killed her. He didn't, did he?" Jean looked at her with open trusting eyes.

Kim felt a lump form in her throat. "No, honey, he did not. Bert is going to find out who really is guilty."

"And you're helping her?" The innocent, cherubic face broke Kim's heart.

"I'm doing my best. Honor bright."

Jean gave her a quick hug. "Okay. I want to watch some more TV now."

"Sure. I'll go talk to your sister."

Kim found Evie in the bedroom she was sharing with her sister. It had a stark, masculine look. There were football posters on the walls likely belonging to one of the boys. Now Evie's cousins had to share a bedroom as well. Evie was working on a laptop when Kim entered the room. She looked up.

"I'm trying to do my homework on this old computer. Aunt Louise took us to school. We had to register because we don't know when we're going home. It really sucks!"

"It does," Kim agreed. "You learned something about life. It isn't fair."

Evie let out a snort. "I knew that years ago. So when can I have my computer back?"

Kim sat down on one of the beds. "Bert has it now. It's evidence for your Dad's defense. She'll take good care of it."

"I hope so. Jerry's computer is an old hunk of junk."

"Evie, can I ask you a favor?"

"Depends." Kim saw the girl was in a surly mood.

"Your sister's suffering, just like you are. Jean is young and really needs her big sister's help and support."

"Like I'm not suffering? Please!" Evie pushed her hair back in a furious motion.

"Of course, you are. But this horrible situation might be easier if you and your sister reached out to each other."

Evie rose to her feet. "Jean's such a baby. She still thinks Evelyn came back because she loved us and missed us."

"Maybe it would be best not to discuss that with her. Look, when Jean was little and your dad put money under her pillow and took her tooth, did you tell your sister there was no such thing as the tooth fairy?"

"No, I didn't."

"Why?"

"I didn't want to ruin it for her."

"Well, think of your mother as the tooth fairy or Santa Claus. Let your sister keep her illusions a little longer. Allow her to hold on to her childhood beliefs for the moment. Life is hard enough."

Evie lowered her eyes. "I don't know if that's right."

"I'm often wrong, but not about this. Evie, tonight before you and Jean go to sleep, give you sister a hug and tell her you love her."

Evie shrugged, reluctant.

"Do it for your dad's sake," Kim urged.

"Oh, all right. I guess I could."

Kim squeezed her hand. "Good girl. You'll feel better too."

"Maybe."

"I've been thinking. Did your mother have any close friends that you remember?"

The girl closed her eyes for a moment. "There was Carol. She and Evelyn used to be friends, but that was before she left. They would laugh together a lot I remember. But one day they had this argument. I never saw Carol again."

"Do you remember Carol's last name?"

"It was Dodd. Mr. Dodd installed a new central air conditioning unit for us when the old one went. He was pretty nice. Evelyn liked him too."

"Are the Dodds still in Webster Township?"

"I guess. Evelyn used to go to the beauty parlor where Carol worked. But we haven't been there in years." Evie paused. "I don't think Carol would know anything about what happened to Evelyn."

"Were there any other friends of your mother that you remember? Anyone more recent?"

Evie bit her lower lip. "Sorry, I just can't think of anyone. After Evelyn came back, I stayed away from home as much as I could. We didn't talk to each other. It was like we were strangers."

Kim saw Evie's pained expression and felt sympathy. "I had a similar relationship with Carl Reyner, the man who was supposed to be my father. I understand how you feel."

"Do you?"

"Yes, I really do. You might feel better if you start reaching out to others. Jean in particular. Also how about helping out your aunt? She didn't sign on to take care of four kids. You could help with meals and cleaning up."

"I do help." Color rose to Evie's cheeks. "Well, not all the time."

"I think she'd appreciate it, even if she doesn't ask."

"Okay. I have to finish my homework now. This school's even worse than my old one. They think kids are slave labor."

"I hope to see you again soon."

"Yeah, me too," Evie said.

Kim closed the door on her way out. She found Louise Gardner in the kitchen relaxing with a cup of tea.

"Want one?" Louise offered raising her cup.

"No, I'm good. I just wanted to ask you what you knew about your sister-in-law."

Louise looked at her in surprise. "Me? I hardly knew Evelyn at all."

"Anything might help. I'm just trying to collect some information. You never know what might be useful."

"I do want to help," Louise said. She looked tired and Kim was reluctant to bother the woman.

"Did you go to high school with Evelyn?"

"Not exactly. She was a senior when I was a freshman. But I knew who she was because she was a cheerleader and very popular."

"Did you happen to know Carol Dodd?"

"I met her and her husband at Mike's house once or twice. Carol's a hairdresser in Webster. She used to work at a shop called the Clip Joint. She could still work there."

"Would you know any of Evelyn's other friends, past or present?"

Louise shook her head. "We weren't that close. It was Mike we saw often and the girls, especially after Evelyn left. We didn't even discuss her. I'm sorry not to be more helpful."

Chapter Thirty-Four

Bert was pleased that she'd been able to wrap up the burglary case quickly. Lyle Kruger followed the same M.O. before and after he'd served time. He hadn't even left the area. Not the swiftest criminal she'd ever dealt with. The dumbest one of all had been the robber who'd hit the same convenience store three times, didn't wear a mask or disguise and used his own car for the getaway. Didn't take a rocket scientist to catch that crook. Generally speaking, criminals weren't too bright.

However, when she got back to her desk at headquarters, a whole new set of case files was piled on top of her desk. More busy work. More crap intended to keep her away from the two murder investigations that really mattered. Across the room, she saw Drew Mitchell looking in her direction and snickering. Her hands balled into fists. She itched to punch him.

Mitchell had the nerve to saunter over to her. "I think you took something that belongs in the evidence locker."

"And what would that be?"

"You removed a computer that came from the Gardner house."

"You mean the one you overlooked and left at the house? Little Evie Gardner's personal computer? The one I personally brought in but no tech had time to examine?" They were nose to nose now.

"It was at the crime scene. You shouldn't have touched it. But I'll overlook that. We need it back. It could be important. You had no right to remove it from police headquarters once it was logged into the evidence locker."

"You forget I was the one who brought it there in the first place."

"Well, bring it back."

"When the captain tells me to, I will." She stood, hands on hips.

"You're a real pain in the butt," Mitchell said. "I don't like your disrespectful attitude."

"I respect people who deserve it," she said. "I don't kiss ass. By the way, your investigation of the Gardner case, isn't that a conflict of interest?"

Mitchell frowned. "What do you mean?"

"You dated Evelyn."

His eyes widened. "You're talking about back in high school?"

"Didn't you also have a relationship with her after she was married?"

"You don't know what you talking about."

"Think so? There's reason to believe Evelyn could have been blackmailing some people. Maybe you were one of them." Bert stood back and watched as her words sunk in.

Mitchell worked to control himself. "You better watch what you say. You could find yourself in a lot of trouble. I can bring you plenty of grief." He pointed his index finger as if it were a loaded pistol.

"You think you can frighten me? Forget it! Ain't gonna happen. Oh, and yeah, I'll check out my car before I get into it. I haven't forgotten how you warned Gardner not to go out to the parking lot right before the mayor's car blew up. A little fun and games for the chief? You a member of his special goon squad, his personal stooge? Don't bother to deny it. One of these days it's going to catch up with you. Like they say: what comes around goes around."

"In your dreams, bitch!"

Bert stood to her full height, back ramrod straight. "Everybody knows how the chief and the mayor went at it, the mayor accusing the chief of corruption and asking him to resign. Anything happens to me, I know who to blame. And I'm not afraid. I always carry." She indicated her holstered service weapon attached to her utility belt. "Oh, and better watch *your* mouth. You wouldn't want to be brought up on charges of sexual harassment or racial discrimination." Bert grabbed her jacket and several of the new files from her desk then stalked out of the office.

She walked out to her car and sat there for several minutes steaming. She'd meant what she said. He'd be sorry if he messed with her. Her cell phone was ringing. It took a minute for her to notice.

"St. Croix here," she said as soon as she'd flipped the cell open.

"Hi, you angry?" She recognized Fred Lincoln's voice.

"Sorry, just had a confrontation with the detective who arrested Gardner."

"You might not want to make an enemy of him."

"Too late for that," she said.

"The thing is we can use all the information we can get for the defense."

"Honestly, I don't think we were going to get anything from Drew Mitchell regardless. He was never planning to be cooperative."

"Sorry to hear that," the attorney said.

"Did you phone for a particular reason?"

"I want to talk with you about the case. Can we do it over dinner tonight?"

She hoped he wasn't pushing for a date. Getting involved with Gardner's lawyer didn't seem like a smart idea. She hesitated, trying to think of a way to refuse that wouldn't tick him off.

"It's okay if you can't make it. But I really think it would be good for both of us to talk in a more relaxed setting. It might help me do a more thorough job."

"Okay, your persuasive argument has won," Bert said.

"You know Berlini's in downtown New Brunswick?"

"No, but I'm sure I can find it."

"Great Italian food. You like Italian?"

"I'm not fussy about food."

"Well, it happens I am," Lincoln said.

They made up to meet at 7 p.m. As Bert started the car and put on the heat, she questioned if it was a mistake to have dinner with the lawyer. Then she decided to work on her files and not over-think things.

• • •

"You're my last appointment of the day," Carol Dodd said to Kim.

"I'm glad you could fit me in."

"I had a cancellation, hon."

Kim didn't like it when beauticians called her hon. Somehow it seemed to be demeaning when you were pushing thirty. Just one of many reasons she didn't often go to beauty parlors.

"So what do you want done?"

"Just a trim." She studied Carol Dodd, who was a walking advertisement for hair dye. Carol's color was Jean Harlow platinum. Her makeup had been applied with a heavy hand.

"We'll get your hair washed and then I'll give you a cut." Carol narrowed her gaze. "You got good hair, nice and thick. You should be doing more with it. I got product that will make your hair shine, bring out those auburn highlights, and you need makeup. What about your nails? You want them done?"

Kim looked down at Carol Dodd's long vermillion finger nails. "No, it wouldn't be convenient," she replied, not certain what else to say. "I'm on computers a good part of the day. Short nails are best for me."

"Okay, suit yourself."

Kim looked around the beauty parlor as she waited for her hair wash. It was nondescript. She supposed Evelyn had been a customer here at one time. Why had the two women argued? Had the hostility carried over after Evelyn returned from California? She thought about it as the young woman in charge of washing hair placed a black plastic sheet around her.

After the wash, Kim waited while Carol put the finishing touches on a set for an elderly woman. She teased and sprayed hair colored champagne blond. The woman, well into her seventies, smiled and placed folded bills into Carol's uniform pocket.

"You always do a wonderful job," the woman gushed.

"Thanks, Mrs. Daly."

THE BAD WIFE

Carol turned to Kim. "You're next."

As Kim settled into the newly vacated chair, she tried to think how to talk to Carol Dodd about Evelyn Gardner. Now that she was here, Kim was reluctant to bring up the subject.

Carol studied Kim's hair with a critical eye. "When was the last time you had a professional cut?"

"Not in a long time." She wasn't going to explain to this hairdresser that she disliked going to beauty parlors, disliked the hairspray odor and the fuss.

"Well, it shows. You need work on your hair to show it to advantage. I'll do what I can. Give you a more up-to-date look." Carol began cutting her hair using a razor.

Kim felt alarmed but tried to keep calm. She was reminded of Samson being shorn of strength by Delilah. Well, that was a silly thought, wasn't it? Time to speak up, no matter how difficult.

Kim cleared her throat. "I'm a friend of Michael Gardner," she said.

Carol stopped cutting and looked at her. "Yeah? Why would that interest me?"

"I thought it might. Evie, Mike's daughter, mentioned that you used to be friends with her mother."

The hairdresser's expression was none too friendly. "That friendship was over a long time ago." She gave a yank at the side of Kim's hair.

"Ouch!"

"Did that hurt? Sorry, just straightening out the length."

"That's all right. I didn't mean to upset you. I was just wondering about something."

Carol's mouth tightened. "What was that?"

"Well, Evie said you and her mother argued. May I ask what you argued about? It must have been serious to break up a longstanding friendship."

"Why do you want to know?"

"You may have heard that Mike's been arrested for killing Evelyn. He didn't do it."

Carol looked around. The shop was empty now except for the two of them. Carol seated herself on the chair next to Kim. "If you must know, Evelyn betrayed our friendship in the worst way possible."

"Could you please explain? I'm not being nosy. I'm trying to find anything that might help Mike."

"I can't see how this would help him. But it's not exactly a secret. Evelyn and me, we were good friends for many years. We were like sisters. Then I caught her in my house in my bed with my husband. I couldn't believe it! I kicked her out, the skanky whore! As for my husband, I made him grovel like a dog for my forgiveness. I was ready to divorce him. But he swore up and down that Evelyn came on to him. Claimed he knew he'd made a big mistake and nothing like that would happen ever again. We have three kids. He was a good dad. I didn't want the kids to grow up without him in their lives. So I forgave him eventually. But the truth is it's never been the same between us. Once trust is gone, you don't have much else left."

Kim understood. "Did Mike ever find out about it?"

"I don't know. I don't think so. She had him snowed. I didn't tell Mike, and neither did Bob, my husband. Evelyn used to complain about Mike being too busy with his job and how he cared more for the girls than her. She had a big ego and it needed constant feeding. It hurt to think I never really knew her." Carol rose from the chair. "Come on. I'll finish your haircut. It's getting late."

"All right. Thank you for telling me."

"Yeah, well like I said, I don't think it's going to help Mike."

Chapter Thirty-Five

Berlini's was nestled in the business section of New Brunswick. It was a small restaurant off the main drag. The elderly waiter who seated them wore a big gray mustache and appeared to know Fred Lincoln.

"So what do you like?" Lincoln asked, studying his menu.

Bert had glanced at the menu, but her mind floated elsewhere.

"I'm no gourmet," she said. "To me Italian food is pizza, ravioli, meatballs and spaghetti or lasagna."

"Well, all of that is great," he said, "but how about living dangerously? What would you say to chicken cacciatore or maybe veal Marsala?"

"Dangerous is how I live," she replied.

He took her hand in his. "I'm glad to hear that."

"You wouldn't be flirting with me, would you?"

"Got that right." His eyes twinkled.

The waiter arrived with a basket of bread. He took their orders and then came back with the wine Fred requested. The waiter poured a little wine into Fred's glass. The lawyer tasted it, nodded approval, and the waiter served both of them with a flourish. She noted that Fred seemed more at home with the niceties than she did.

"I like a full-bodied dark wine," he told her in a soft voice, leaning forward to clink glasses.

She choked on the wine, interrupting the intimate moment. Just as well because she wasn't certain how to respond. Glib talk wasn't easy for her.

She said, "So I believe we're meeting to discuss Mike Gardner's defense."

"That's one reason."

"I have a problem," she said.

"And what would that be?"

"I didn't return Evie's computer to headquarters. Drew Mitchell asked for it."

Fred took a sip of wine looking thoughtful. "You're afraid he'll try to delete information?"

"I am."

"You and Ms. Reynolds made copies of every important piece of information, didn't you?"

"I think we need more time. There were a lot of emails."

"Okay. Warn Mitchell that all the information on the machine has been backed up. So if anything is deleted, he'll be questioned about it in court. That ought to put the fear of God into him. In any case, you're going to have to return the computer tomorrow."

"All right, I accept that."

"Good, that's a step in the right direction."

The waiter served their salads and for a while they ate in companionable silence.

Fred Lincoln studied her with a puzzled look.

"What?"

"I understand why Ms. Reynolds is knocking herself out to help free Gardner. But what's in it for you?"

Bert put down her fork. "I was feeling depressed and confused when I left New York to take this job in snoburbia. Didn't think it was going to work out for me. Thought I might have made a big mistake. Mike was supportive and so was Kim. I consider them both friends."

"And you're loyal to your friends. I get that."

"What about you? Why did you become a lawyer?"

"Hard to say exactly. I was born in Newark. Got to see the mean streets first-hand. A cousin of mine was murdered for no reason. Lots of senseless violence. My parents had enough. They moved to a safer place where they didn't have to worry about us kids so much."

"Working in Webster's taught me there's no such thing as a safe place. But I'd like to think I'm helping."

"My feelings as well."

"You didn't answer my question about why you became a lawyer."

"Okay, I've always been fascinated by the legal system. I started reading mystery and crime stories, real and fictional, back in middle school. Must have read and reread *Crime and Punishment* any number of times. I knew early on practicing law was what I wanted to do for a living."

"Why not become a prosecutor?" she asked.

He shrugged. "It just wasn't a good fit for me. I always thought of the people that might be convicted unjustly. I want to make certain that everyone has the best representation possible, innocent or guilty."

"I don't like the idea that criminals go free because they have a slick lawyer."

"I don't deny it can happen. However, the system usually works."

"I'll try to take your word for it."

"But I haven't convinced you?" He tilted his head to one side.

"Afraid not."

"Why did you choose me to defend Gardner?"

"I asked around. I was told the judges have a lot of respect for you. That's not typical."

"I do my best," he said.

"And you're modest."

"Only when I'm trying to impress a sexy lady."

She felt uncomfortable. "Did you like law school?"

"Don't get me started on that topic. No, I didn't like law school one bit. You don't learn how to be a lawyer until you start to practice. It's a very impractical form of education."

"Ditto being a cop," she said. "Kim said the same thing about teaching."

"As Ben Franklin said, 'Experience is the best teacher.' A toast to pragmatists everywhere."

They raised their glasses and clinked in silent agreement.

"Hope you're not trying to get me drunk," she said.

He gave her an innocent look. "Me? Wouldn't think of it. You're too sharp to let that happen anyway."

"Yeah, you're a very good lawyer all right. Smooth as a baby's ass."

Fred laughed and raised his glass to her again.

Chapter Thirty-Six

Kim decided she hadn't learned much from Carol Dodd. The hairdresser only confirmed what Kim already knew: Evelyn Gardner had cheated on her husband.

After finishing a light dinner, Kim picked up Evelyn's diary, settled on the sofa, and began to read. The early pages were what she would expect from a teenager: talk of clothes, boys, dances, and dates. It began in Evelyn's freshman year of high school. The entries were sporadic. Kim's eyelids began to droop.

She awoke with a start. Her cell phone was ringing. She groped around for a moment and found the cell in her handbag.

"You took your time answering," Bert said.

"Sorry. I forgot where I left my phone."

"You sound groggy. You okay?"

"I drifted off for a bit. I'm awake now though."

"I thought we should compare notes," Bert said.

"I agree." She proceeded to tell Bert about Carol Dodd.

Bert listened without interrupting until Kim finished. "I don't think she was a fan of Evelyn's, but I don't get a sense of her being a murderer, although for a while there I thought she might scalp me."

Bert laughed. "Can't mess with beauticians when they got their hands on your hair. Get anything else from Dodd?"

"There is one thing. Carol said she caught her husband in bed with Evelyn. Both Dodds decided to blame the whole sordid business on Evelyn the seductress. So I wonder. What if Evelyn decided to reconnect with Dodd when she came back to town? If he was sleeping with Evelyn again and she tried to blackmail him, he might have killed her."

"Maybe I'll have a little talk with Dodd," Bert said.

"I was going to try to find out where he works tomorrow."

"I'll take care of it. I might get more info from him than you would."

"All right," Kim said. "Meantime, I'll get back to reading Evelyn's diary."

"Anything of interest?"

"Not so far. It put me to sleep. But there's plenty more to read. I'll get back to it."

"Okay. Talk to you tomorrow. And Kim, let me know if you get a vision that will solve this case."

"I'll let you know, but I don't control those things."

Kim tried to make progress in the diary, but she couldn't concentrate. Finally she put the book down and set her alarm for an hour earlier than usual. In the morning she would try again with a clear, sharp mind.

She dreamed of Mike. She drifted into the prison and sat beside him on the bunk in his cell.

"You've come," he said. He touched her cheek, but she could not feel it.

"How did I get here?"

"I called you to me. I needed for us to be together. It will give me the strength to endure this ordeal. I knew you wouldn't mind."

"I wish we could really be together," she said.

"We are. We'll always be connected."

Kim looked around her. "This is such a terrible place, so sterile, so isolated."

"Sweetheart, as long as long as I have you, it won't matter where I am."

"But this is just a dream. We aren't together in reality."

"Who's to say? Dreams are part of reality."

"I hope you're right," she said.

Mike caressed her cheek and kissed her lips. "We'll be together soon."

"I want us to be together again," Kim said, "the way we were before Evelyn came back."

"I want that too. I want to make love to you again."

And then when she reached for Mike, he was gone and she was terrified. He was in danger. She needed to warn him. But the connection was lost. She was awake, soaked in sweat and shaking with cold.

She glanced at the clock radio. Four in the morning. She wouldn't sleep again tonight.

With a mug of green tea beside her, she tackled the diary again. She started again from the beginning. She read the details about Evelyn's mother. Sheila Cooper had died of cancer, a long, lingering, painful death. Evelyn's older sister had assumed responsibility for most of their mother's care. She left home immediately after Sheila died. Evelyn was sixteen and dating Mike.

> "I'm crazy about Mike. He's the quarterback, the most important player on the football team. He's so popular. When I'm with him, all the girls envy me. It's so cool!"

That was telling. Kim wondered if Evelyn ever really loved Mike. To her he seemed to represent a status symbol.

Kim examined more pages. Later that year Evelyn observed:

> "It's so great being a cheerleader. Everyone thinks I'm totally hot. I want things to stay like this forever. I'm going to try out for a part in the drama club's play too. Wish I had more time for everything."

Kim reflected that her own high school years hadn't been much fun. Obviously, Evelyn loved being the center of attention, while Kim had been quiet and bookish. She certainly hadn't been popular or even aspired to be. How strange that Mike could love two such different women.

Was there anything of substance in the diary? The next few pages were just more of the same shallow dribble. Evelyn sounded like a typical teenage girl. Kim was ready to put the diary down for dark bold print caught her attention.

> **"DADDY CAME INTO MY ROOM LAST NIGHT.** He said he was sad and lonely now that Maryann left us and Mom was gone. He said he needed me to make things right for him. I didn't know what he meant at first. It was a shock when he unzipped his pants and insisted I touch him. I told Daddy I knew it wasn't right. He got angry and said it was, said Maryann did what he told her to do and I wasn't going to be any different. I was getting too full of myself."

Kim saw there was a blank page. The next entry was several days later.

> "Daddy came home from work and told me to get dinner on the table. I told him I'd already eaten pizza with some of the kids after cheerleading practice. He got angry and said now that Maryann had left us it was my turn to take over her duties. He called me a spoiled brat. I went to my room and locked the door. Later on he started banging at the door. I didn't want to let him in. I told him I wasn't feeling well. That wasn't a lie. He was making me feel sick. Daddy kicked in my door. I never saw him behave that way. It was awful. He smelled like liquor. He wanted me to touch him and other yucky stuff I don't want to describe. After a while, I told him I had to use the bathroom and locked myself in there until he finally went back to his own room. I don't know what to do. He's acting so weird. Should I tell someone? But who?"

Kim felt sick. She hadn't considered that Evelyn might have been sexually abused. She wondered if Mike had some inkling. The next entry was even worse.

"Daddy forced me to have sex with him last night. It was horrible. I was crying but he didn't care. He said because he used a condom there was nothing wrong with it. But I don't think that's true. He warned me not to tell anyone because if I did they'd take me away. So Diary, I'm not telling anyone else. Not even Mike. He probably wouldn't want me to be his girlfriend anymore if he knew. All those girls and boys who think I'm special would think I was trash if they found out the truth. If I report Daddy to Mrs. Fergus my guidance counselor, she might find a way to make him stop. She'd call the police or child welfare. But then everyone would know and I'd be humiliated. They'd throw Daddy in jail. Where would I live? Everyone would say I was dirt. I couldn't stand the shame. Why did Maryann have to go away? I hate her now."

Kim closed the diary, appalled. She thought about her own childhood and adolescence. She'd been verbally and emotionally abused by Carl Reyner, but there hadn't been anything of this nature, nothing sexual. She recalled the poem "Richard Cory" by Edwin Arlington Robinson. She supposed you never knew from outward appearance what others suffered in their lives or how they would react.

She found herself feeling sorry for Evelyn, for the young girl who'd had her innocence stolen.

Chapter Thirty-Seven

Bert found Robert Dodd working at a construction site. After she told him who she was and flashed her I.D., Dodd's face turned pale. Bert didn't want to come on too strong. She managed a small smile.

"I was told you were in heating and air conditioning," she said.

"Yeah, I am. Our company's going to do it for every townhouse that will be built here."

Bert glanced around. Men were working with construction equipment all around her. "How many units are going in?"

"Forty-eight all together."

"Great that your company's doing so well," she said.

"Yeah, well, we weren't for quite a while there. Whole industry's been in the toilet. But I think it's starting to come back again. Least I hope so. Sick to death of the lousy economy. Anyway, the units won't be going up until spring. Weather's getting too cold for the men to work out here."

"Mr. Dodd, I guess you're wondering why a police detective is visiting you on your job."

He took his hard hat off, wiped sweat from his forehead, though the temperature was near freezing.

"Something to do with Evelyn Gardner?"

"That's right."

"I'm gonna tell you straight out. I haven't seen her in years."

"But you had an affair with Evelyn Gardner before she left for L.A., didn't you?"

His eyes shifted away from her. "It wasn't an affair. Just a one-night stand. I screwed up and I know it. Carol and I don't like to be reminded. My wife forgave me. I never did anything so stupid again."

"You were friends of both Evelyn and Michael Gardner?"

"Mostly, Evelyn and Carol were friends. They'd been friends since high school. Evelyn said Mike wasn't around much and she was lonely. Carol worked long hours too. I'd been laid off at the time and felt pretty low myself. People make mistakes. Over and done with. Now if you'll excuse me, I have work to do."

He stalked away.

She watched him go. She was pretty sure she had gotten only part of the truth at most. This was one nervous fella, and not a very bright one if he thought he could lie to a cop. If she jacked him up, would he be able to account for his whereabouts at the time of Evelyn's death?

Kim phoned Bert at headquarters that afternoon.

"What's up?" she asked.

"I was going through Evelyn's diary early this morning. I didn't get too far before I got hit with a shocker."

"What kind of a shocker?"

"I can't find a place that isn't crowded with students right now, and I want to talk about this with you privately."

"Okay, you want to meet me at the Galaxy when you get off work?"

"Sure, that would be fine."

Bert concentrated on demolishing some of the paperwork in front of her. She couldn't help noticing that Drew Mitchell hadn't been in the office all afternoon. She had a bad feeling the sneaky bastard was up to something that wouldn't be good for Mike.

The Galaxy Lounge was quiet when Bert arrived. It was early for the regulars to show up. She saw that Kim had already arrived and was talking with April Nevins.

April smiled as Bert slid into the booth opposite Kim. "Just in time to give me your drink order," April said.

"I'm having glass of Merlot," Kim said.

"You want the same?" April asked.

"I'm not technically off duty yet so just bring me some cran juice."

"Got it." April did a slow assessing look at Kim's hair. "What happened? That cut isn't you."

Kim's hand went up. "I was razor cut by an unfriendly beautician."

"Next time you want to get your hair done, ask me," April said. "I've got this great hairdresser. You might have noticed my trademark blond highlights? They look natural, don't they? One thing I don't stint on is my hair. It's a woman's glory."

"I'll keep that in mind," Kim said in a dry voice.

"I'll get you some nuts and pretzels so you can nibble." April took off with a slow, sexy walk that had the men in the place following her with their eyes.

Bert leaned forward. "Amazing how she does that without even trying."

Kim nodded. "We could both learn a thing or two from April."

"You bet." Bert studied Kim's hair.

"What do you think?"

She shrugged. "Not so bad, just different."

"Not my style?"

"Not really. But the Dodd woman didn't do a bad job. And it grows back."

"Thanks for the comforting words. Speaking of the Dodds, I meant to ask you how things went with Mr. Dodd."

"He swore he hadn't seen Evelyn since she came back."

"Did you believe him?"

"No."

"So you consider him a suspect?"

"Sure do," Bert said. "Okay, what's your shocker?"

"First, I'm not a prude."

"Never said you were."

"Okay. According to the diary, Evelyn's father molested her. He started when she turned sixteen, after her mother died and the older sister took off. I think he was forcing big sister Maryann to have sex with him. She ran off after the mother died."

Bert scowled. "Damn, the older one should have pressed charges against him. I can't believe she allowed the same thing to happen to her younger sister. She must have realized it would."

"I feel guilty for disliking Evelyn so much."

"Well, I don't. I didn't like her either. She was a nasty piece of work. The fact that she came from a screwed-up family doesn't change that."

April returned with the snacks. "What's wrong?" she asked.

"It's this case, Evelyn Gardner's murder. I don't know if we're getting anywhere with it," Bert said.

"I think we need to get in touch with Evelyn's father and sister," Kim said.

Bert nodded. "I'll take care of it. Mike probably kept their addresses in his book. I'll check."

"Wouldn't Detective Mitchell have informed them of Evelyn's death?"

Bert raised her eyes to the planet paintings on the ceiling. "Since I had my ass officially kicked off the case, I haven't consulted with Mitch. Had I been on the case, I'd have attended Evelyn's funeral and made a note of those present."

"I'll talk to Louise and the girls. They'll know who else was there."

"Can't hurt," Bert said.

"I'd like to help too," April said. "Anything I can do, just let me know."

"Thank you," Kim said.

The bartender came toward them. "April, this ain't your break time. Get your ass moving."

Bert stood and turned a stern look on the bartender. "I'm discussing police business with your waitress. This isn't a social call. You got a problem with that?"

"Guess not." He gave a small, nervous salute and headed back to the safety of his bar.

April snickered. "God, I love it when Bert gets tough. Frankie is such bastard, always harassing us waitresses."

"Let me know if he continues to bother you," Bert said. "I hate bullies, especially the kind that pick on women."

"I'll be right back with your drinks," April said.

Chapter Thirty-Eight

Kim visited Chuck and Louise Gardner's home the following evening. She realized she could have phoned, but she wanted to see Evie and Jean to find out how they were doing. Chuck greeted her at the door. He looked like a somewhat younger version of Mike. They both had gray eyes and wavy brown black hair. Both men were tall, lean, well-muscled. But there were differences. She got no sense that Chuck had much insight into people.

"Come right in," Chuck said. "Cold out there tonight."

"Yes, they're forecasting possible snow overnight."

Chuck rubbed his hands together. "I hope not. Traveling in snow's a real pain. My boys would be happy though for a day off school."

Kim placed her wool coat into Chuck's outstretched hands. "I guess the girls wouldn't mind a day off either."

A shadow crossed Chuck's face. "No, they wouldn't mind. This whole business has been hard on them. And adjusting to a new school, trying to fit in, it's not easy either."

They were joined by Louise who wiped her hands on a floral apron. Louise's hair was pulled back in a ponytail. Her complexion was rosy from the kitchen heat, and she looked almost youthful.

"Kim, good to see you again. We're just finishing dinner but there's plenty of food left. Why don't you join us? You look like you could stand to gain a few pounds."

"If it wouldn't be too much trouble, I'd love to join you."

At the table a plate of baked chicken, broccoli and mashed yams was placed in front of her. Kim hadn't realized she was hungry until she saw the food. Louise sat beside Kim. Everyone else was finished with dinner and had taken off in different directions.

"I came to visit with the girls and also to talk with you about

Evelyn's funeral," Kim said, "—although it must look to you as if I came to get another free meal. You are a very good cook."

Louise smiled. "You compliment my culinary ability, you're welcome here anytime. As for Evelyn's funeral, maybe you and I should discuss that right now. It's better if the girls aren't involved. They were both awfully upset."

"I agree," Kim said. "Can you tell me who was at the cemetery?"

"Well, it was poorly attended. There was Chuck and myself of course and the children. We let our boys go to school. They didn't know their aunt."

"Who else was there? Was Detective Mitchell present?"

"Was he the one who came around asking questions?"

"I suppose so," Kim said.

"I didn't see him at the funeral. Was he supposed to be there?"

"Not necessarily." Kim knew that if Bert had been in charge of the investigation, she would have been at the cemetery.

Louise said, "Let me think. There were a few people who I believe went to school with Evelyn, but I'm not exactly sure who they were."

"Men or women?"

"Both. It was very cold and the graveside service was brief. I really didn't know who was there. I didn't ask any names or anything."

"Would Chuck know?"

"You can ask him but I don't think so. He was younger than Mike and Evelyn. They didn't share any of the same friends. And then Mike was away in the service for a while."

"Okay, I'll just ask Chuck to make certain."

Kim helped Louise clear the table and rinse the dishes. For a time, they worked in companionable silence.

Kim said, "Louise, did you ever meet Evelyn's sister or her father?"

"No, I didn't. They weren't around when Chuck and I started dating."

Chuck entered the kitchen. "I'm ready for dessert," he said. "Need any help?"

"That's all right. Kim will help me. You can gather up the children."

"Sounds like a plan." When he smiled, a dimple appeared that reminded Kim of Mike's. It made her heart ache.

"Chuck, before you go," Kim said, "do you remember Evelyn's sister or her father?"

"Sure. Our family paid a condolence call when Evelyn's mother passed away."

"What impressions did you have of them?"

Chuck rolled up the sleeves of his plaid flannel shirt, his eyes considering. "It was such a long time ago and I was really just a kid. I thought Mike didn't much like either one of them, but he was polite and civil. The sister wasn't pretty like Evelyn, maybe because she was on the heavy side. She looked miserable, but then how would anyone feel under those circumstance? The father, I don't know. He had big biceps, light-colored hair and blue eyes like Evelyn's. He kept putting his arms around both girls. I guess he must have loved them a lot."

Too much, Kim thought.

"Did you see either of them at Evelyn's funeral?"

"No, I don't recall them being there. They might not have even known about it."

"You didn't attempt to reach them by phone?"

Chuck and Louise exchanged embarrassed looks. Louise said, "You know there was so much going on around here. Neither one of us thought of it, I'm ashamed to say."

"That's all right. The police will inform them," Kim said.

Evie walked into the kitchen. When she saw Kim, her face lit up. "Kim, I'm so glad you came to visit us. Have you seen my dad?"

"Sorry, dear, I haven't been allowed. So far only his lawyer has talked to him."

"It's so unfair!" Tears formed in Evie's eyes. "I want to see my dad."

Kim hugged the sobbing girl.

"It's going to be all right. Detective St. Croix is working hard to find the person who really killed your mother. Your dad will be free soon." She spoke with more confidence than she felt. Her dream about Mike had left an unpleasant resonance.

Evie pulled away, eyes wide with fear. "But what if he's not? What if they convict him?"

"They won't," Kim said firmly. "Stay strong. Your dad needs you to be strong and so does Jean. She looks up to you."

Evie looked at the floor. "I'll try. But I've made up my mind. If my dad goes to trial, I'm going to go to court and tell them I killed Evelyn. I hated her. I could have killed her."

"Don't think that way. It's going to be all right."

"But you can't promise, can you?"

"No," she admitted, "I can't promise."

Kim begged off dessert.

As she got into her car, once again she felt she was being watched. Driving home, she glanced repeatedly at the rear view mirror but saw no one close. Was she suffering from paranoia? She couldn't be sure.

She wished there was someone she could confide in. But if she told even a friend like Bert about the dream—with its disturbing image of Mike fading away—the police detective would decide she was a few slices short of a loaf. Kim had spent her life pretending she was ordinary. She dressed plainly, wore little makeup or jewelry. She didn't want to be noticed. But she and Mike *did* share a psychic awareness. She'd known he sensed it when they first met, just as she did. His innate sensitivity told him that she had repressed her sixth sense, just as she'd repressed her sexuality.

It was a cold and lonely drive home.

Chapter Thirty-Nine

Bert was at her desk bright and early the following morning. She decided to ignore the mound of paperwork. A lot of the old cases were petty crimes. Busy work.

This morning she had collected Mike Gardner's address book from his house. Now she took it out and examined it.

Drew Mitchell approached and she quickly dropped the book in a drawer.

"Where's that laptop from Gardner's house?"

"Been so overworked I forgot all about it."

Mitchell stared at her with overt disgust. "I don't want to have to bring this to the captain's attention."

"Have it for you tomorrow."

"You better."

Bert studied the detective. Mitchell was in his middle to late thirties but looked older. His hair was thinning and he had a beer gut. She hoped he ate himself to death at the local donut shop, but in the meantime she planned to avoid confrontations with him.

Her cell phone rang and she caught it on the first ring. "St. Croix."

"Bert, it's Kim. I took my break early so we could compare notes."

"I'm at my desk."

"So you have to be careful what you say?"

"You got it."

"Did you find the address book?"

"Affirmative."

"Good. I visited Mike's family. Louise told me that as far as she knows neither Evelyn's sister nor her father attended the funeral. I think Detective Mitchell failed to inform them."

"I think you're right," Bert said. "Mighty sloppy police work." She watched Mitchell as she spoke. He was looking pleased with himself about something. He wouldn't be for long.

"So you'll contact them?"

"That's my intention."

"Good. Let me know what you discover."

"Right." Bert closed her phone. She retrieved the address book and slipped it into her pocket, gathered a bunch of the file folders and left the office. It had snowed overnight, not heavily but enough to make the roads slippery. Bert decided to drive back to her apartment, where she would be assured privacy. Her small apartment was in a complex right off the main highway. They were called garden apartments, but even in the summer nothing there reminded of her a garden. She'd rented because of the convenience to the civic center complex. When she let herself in, she glanced around the unit and thought she ought to do something about making it presentable. Maybe hang a few posters. Kim had prints of impressionist paintings on the walls of her studio apartment, and they made the small space more cheerful. She could do something similar. Bert realized she hadn't considered doing anything before because she wasn't certain she wanted to stay in this hick town. When you were born, raised, and lived your entire life in New York City, small towns took some getting used to.

Bert raised the thermostat, sat at her table and hunted through Mike's address book until she found the first number she was after. There was only one Maryann; the last name was Cooper. She called and someone answered on the third ring.

"Hello?"

"Is this Maryann Cooper?"

"Yes, it is. Who wants to know?" The woman's tone was tense.

Bert identified herself and then gave Maryann the bad news about her sister. For a few moments there was silence at the other end. "Ms. Cooper, are you all right?"

"It's a shock."

"I'm sorry."

"Don't be. At least not for me. Evelyn and I haven't had any contact since I left town years ago."

"Why was that?"

"We had some harsh words after my mother died. I'd taken on all the responsibility of caring for her for several years. I had no social life while Evelyn enjoyed being a normal teenager. I left my job and stayed at home. I suppose I was jealous."

"But that wasn't why you left so abruptly, was it?"

Silence greeted Bert's question.

"Look, no offense, but that's long over. It's a painful subject. I prefer not to go there with a stranger."

"I understand. But you see, your sister didn't just die, she was murdered. Michael Gardner's been arrested. There are a number of people who believe that's a mistake."

"Mike? He was nice. But I don't see that I can help. Like I told you, I've had no contact with my sister in years."

"She never tried to reach you?"

Large sigh. "No, never."

"Suppose I told you that Evelyn kept a diary and in that diary she wrote that when you left, your father began molesting her. He told her that he used to satisfy his needs with you before you escaped."

"My, God!"

"Does that shock you?"

No answer at the other end. But Maryann clearly hadn't hung up. Bert could hear heavy breathing at the other end.

"Look, I'm sorry to trouble you, except I can't help wondering if what happened to you and your sister might have some relevance to her murder."

"Detective, my father was a disgusting creep, and yes, I did escape. Mentally, I never fully recovered. I don't have any relations with men if I can help it. I'm a hundred pounds overweight. I'm not pretty and I couldn't care less. I'm a graphic artist who does most of her work from home. All I ever wanted was to put my past behind me. I certainly didn't kill my sister. I had no reason to do such a thing." Bert thought the woman did sound both insecure and unhappy. She also sounded like she was telling the truth.

"No one's accusing you. But do you think it's possible that Evelyn might have demanded money from your father to keep his ugly secret?"

"I—I don't know."

"Has he been in contact with you?"

"No, not since I left home. I made it clear I never wanted to see him or hear from him again."

"Evelyn must have known where you were. Mike had your information in his address book. Did you give it to him?"

"No, not at all."

Bert was thoughtful. "Where did you go after you left Webster?"

"My mother had an aunt. I took my savings and a few pieces of jewelry Mom had given me, got a neighbor to give me a lift, and then called my aunt from Philadelphia. She came out and picked me up. She didn't tell my father where I was. I made her promise me she wouldn't."

Bert figured that Mike had probably tracked Maryann down. His innate kindness would have led him to make certain the woman was all right. But he'd decided not to push a reunion between the sisters.

"You still live in Pennsylvania."

"Yes, I went back to school so I could get a college education and make a decent living. My aunt was great. She helped me make a life for myself."

"Did you tell her what your father did to you?"

"No, I was too ashamed. I only told her that he and I weren't getting along."

"She didn't try to get the two of you together, effect reconciliation?"

"No. She never liked my father, thought he wasn't good enough for Mom. I told her she was right."

"You were how old?"

"I'd just turned twenty-one."

"Maryann, you should have gone to the police."

"I couldn't! I was too ashamed. He raped me, made me a sex slave. I just wanted to be free. Please, don't tell anyone."

"If you haven't seen a psychiatrist, you should. You need to confront your problems, not run from them."

"Easy for you to say." Maryann hung up on her.

Bert sat and stared at the empty wall in front of her. How could Maryann have left her younger sister in that kind of a situation? It horrified her.

She picked up the phone, willing herself to punch the number Mike had neatly penned for Lawrence Cooper in Texas. She could barely stand the thought of speaking to the monster. Lucky for him he wasn't here to interrogate in person, because she might very well have beaten him to death with her fists.

She took a series of deep breaths and dialed Lawrence Cooper's number. The telephone rang three times. Then a woman answered.

"Is this the residence of Lawrence Cooper?"

"Yes, it is." The female voice had a Western twang.

"This is Detective Roberta St. Croix. I'm calling from Webster Township, New Jersey in regard to his daughter Evelyn."

"Daughter? What daughter?" The woman sounded puzzled.

"To whom am I speaking?"

"This is Jessica Cooper. I'm Larry's wife."

Bert was now as surprised as Jessica. "Is Mr. Cooper at home?"

"Why yes he is."

"Could you please put him on the phone?"

"Hold on." Footsteps receded.

Bert waited.

"Hello." The man's voice rasped as if he'd smoked one cigarette too many.

"Mr. Lawrence Cooper?"

"That's right." He sounded suspicious.

"I have some bad news for you." She went on to explain what had happened to Evelyn in as sketchy terms as possible.

"Well, this may sound harsh, but she was dead to me long ago.

She went and married that Marine. I told her no good would come of it."

"Did Evelyn contact you recently?"

"No."

"Did she call you and ask you for money?"

"No, I haven't spoken to her in years. Girl was an ungrateful bitch."

"Could that be because you raped her as well as her sister? Did she threaten to finally expose you for the pervert you are if you didn't give her money?"

"How dare you accuse me!"

Explosions of red anger appeared in front of Bert's eyes. She controlled her rage. "We have evidence, Mr. Cooper. Written evidence from your dead daughter. We know what you did to your children. You could go to jail for a very long time."

"Who did you say you were? I'll report you."

"You do that, and tell my captain why I phoned you. We have the evidence to put you away for a very long time."

Bert broke the connection. Let the old bastard sweat. He deserved it He had a good motive for killing Evelyn. She was blackmailing people, hitting them up for money. A creep like Lawrence Cooper who'd molest his own daughters was a good fit for a murderer. In any case, Evelyn's diary would make a fine piece of evidence for Fred Douglas to present. She wondered what else Kim might turn up. Time to do her part and dig through the emails Evelyn left on her daughter's laptop. She had a feeling there could be a number of people who had a motive for murdering Evelyn Gardner.

Chapter Forty

"Do you need some help?" Kim smiled at Don Bernard. The professor looked smart in an Irish sweater and tweeds.

"I thought we might have lunch together today, right now if you can get away. There's something I should discuss with you." His mouth was set in a grave expression. He wasn't trying to flirt with her as he usually did.

"All right. Just let me check with Rita and see if she minds me taking first lunch."

When Rita Mosler saw it was Professor Bernard who waited at the information desk, she was sweetness itself. A person could o.d. on that much saccharine. No problem leaving for lunch.

Kim went and got her coat from the reference office. Ever the gentleman, Don helped her on with it.

"I thought we might dine at the Rathskeller if you don't mind. It's not exactly elegant but I have limited time between classes today and have meetings scheduled with students afterwards."

"We could get together at a more convenient time if you like. It's no problem for me."

"Thank you for offering, but I think now is best."

They were hit by freezing wind as they left the library building. Don took her arm on the icy walkway. They didn't have far to go; the Rat was in the commons building next door. They got their food and sat in the dining room, which was dark and fairly empty.

"How is your work going?" Bernard asked. He was as attractive as ever with his fair hair and light eyes. His smile warmed her.

"I'm happy to be back at the university," she said.

"That's what I wanted to talk to you about. You see, there's been some buzz among faculty about you."

"About me?"

"You are described in a local newspaper article as the lover of the police detective who is under arrest for murdering his wife."

Kim stiffened. "When Evelyn returned to New Jersey, I ended our engagement. Mike thought he was legally divorced. It turned out he wasn't. I did have the misfortune to find Evelyn's body. But I'm certain Mike didn't kill her."

"Sorry, I didn't mean to upset or offend you." Don placed a hand over hers. "I'm concerned for your welfare. I care about you."

Kim removed her hand. "Don, I know you're my friend."

"I'm telling you this just so you realize you need to be careful of your reputation."

"I understand and I appreciate that. And I know you mean well."

"Believe me, I sincerely do. I am and will always be your friend."

She nodded, but she didn't want to encourage any more talk about her reputation. Nor did she feel like small talk. They finished their lunch in a polite but awkward silence. Kim was relieved when Don Bernard glanced at his watch and said he had to dash. She looked down at her salad and realized she'd barely touched it. What she wouldn't say to Don was that she had no intention of deserting Mike no matter what the cost to her personally or professionally.

Out on the street, walking fast, she almost banged into another person. "Sorry," she said.

"Kim, is that you?"

She looked more closely at the other woman. "Vivian, how are you?"

Vivian Laurent, a former classmate of Kim's, gave an embarrassed shrug. "Could be better. I've been working for a cleaning agency. I discovered a latent talent for scrubbing toilets."

"God, I'm sorry." Kim knew Vivian as a dynamic, hard-working fellow student in the library master's degree program. It was sad to think her intellectual abilities were being wasted.

"Remember Jenny Parson?"

"Of course."

"Well, she's pole dancing in Manhattan. Unfortunately, I don't have her attributes." Vivian indicated her own skinny frame.

"Can I do anything to help?" Kim asked.

"I wish you could. I'm back on campus to check the postings and see if any new jobs are available that I can apply for."

"I hope you find something."

Vivian flashed a faint smile that didn't reach her eyes. "That makes two of us. See you around." Vivian walked toward the School of Communication and Information Science.

With a deep sigh, Kim hurried back the rest of the short distance to the humanities library. If they let her go this time, she would likely be joining Vivian. A grim thought. Hard economic times meant fewer jobs for everyone including librarians.

Bert cleared several older case files and decided that would be enough if she was called on it. She left headquarters in a hurry without talking to anyone and went straight to her automobile. She pulled out her cell in the car and phoned Fred Lincoln's office. He picked up on the second ring.

"Hi, Bert," he said. "What's up?"

"Just thought I'd keep you in the loop. Kim discovered some nasty stuff in Evelyn's old diary. Seems her father molested both her and her sister." She was greeted by silence at the other end. "You with me?"

"Sorry, I was just trying to think how that could help our case."

"It's clear to me that Evelyn was after money. Although her father said he hadn't heard from her in years, I'm not so certain that's true. He lives in Texas now, and his phone number was in Mike's book. What if Evelyn threatened to make his behavior public if he didn't cough up some serious cash for her?"

"It's a possibility. I could call him as a witness. But you know, that could backfire."

Bert was puzzled. "How?"

"He'll deny it."

"Yeah, so what? We've got the diary. If necessary, we can subpoena Maryann, his other daughter, to testify."

"What we need is proof that he flew into Jersey from Texas around the time Evelyn was murdered. Just supposition won't do us any good in a courtroom."

"I'll get working on it."

"Anything else?"

"Bob Dodd is another possible candidate. Evelyn had an affair with him back when. I got a feeling it could have been rekindled when she came back to town. He's got a jealous wife. Then there's Mayor Ryan. As I told you, I've got that witness who places him and Evelyn together at the Galaxy Lounge. Ryan also has a jealous wife."

"Seems to be part of being a wife," he said casually.

"I've still got a few other leads to check out as well."

"If this goes to trial, all the evidence will be circumstantial," the lawyer observed. "The more info you collect on Evelyn's amorous pursuits, the more likely we get a jury to vote for reasonable doubt."

"I'm hoping it won't come to that. I'm searching for a murderer and I won't be satisfied until I find him or her."

"Wow, you sound mighty sexy when you're tough and determined."

"I intend to be relentless."

"Glad we're on the same side, detective."

"So am I," she said.

Chapter Forty-One

Kim stopped at the grocery store on the way back to her apartment and picked up a few things. Again she had the sense of being followed. She didn't like it.

Maybe she ought to sign up for a course in self-defense. A class was offered at the adult school in the evenings. She knew a little but not enough. It was important for women to know how to protect themselves.

Kim glanced around before opening the door of her apartment. She didn't see or hear anything out of the ordinary. She carried in her groceries and locked the door behind her. Then she realized her hands were shaking. This was stupid! She refused to live in fear.

She greased a pan with olive oil, rolled the flounder filet she had bought in bread crumbs and paprika and baked it in the oven. There was fresh Italian bread with sesame seeds, nice and crunchy the way she liked it. She tossed packaged salad into a plate, poured, grapefruit juice in a glass and retrieved Evelyn's diary from its hiding place under a sofa cushion. She'd left a bookmark, so it was easy to pick up again.

There was lots of talk about Mike, how smart he was, how athletic, how much a gentleman. In her own way, Kim thought, Evelyn had loved him—at least in the beginning. But as she continued to read, it was painful to learn how Evelyn had pushed Mike into an early marriage, probably before either of them was mature enough to cope with the responsibilities. Evelyn just wanted to escape from her father. She made that clear.

Evelyn didn't go to college, nor did she prepare herself for any particular line of work. She didn't like schoolwork. She stated how boring it was. She looked for work as a sales clerk in a women's clothing store because she loved clothes. But soon that began to bore her as well. Her answer to the problem was to make certain she became pregnant as soon as possible. *"It's going to be such fun,"* she wrote, *"staying at home doing whatever I want."*

Poor Evelyn. It didn't work out as she'd hoped. Kim read:

> *"Little Evie won't stop crying. I try to ignore it but the brat is so loud. I told Mike how miserable I am. He comforts me and says it's hard on all new mothers. I didn't know babies were so much work and trouble. I hate poopy diapers! Mike isn't here enough. He should be home helping me instead of working all the time."*

Kim thought about her own mother. Ma had been kind and patient with her when she was a child. If she was ever fortunate enough to become a mother, she hoped to be as loving and caring as Ma and not self-centered like Evelyn Gardner. It was no surprise that Evie didn't feel a connection to her mother.

Kim forced herself to read on, though she found the diary unpleasant—in fact, downright depressing. Mike, ever considerate, had found a babysitter for Evelyn so she could get out when she wanted. He even suggested she join a local theatre group since she loved acting and idolized film stars.

Kim flipped a few more pages. The entries were at best sporadic. But she found reference to Evelyn's efforts at local theatre.

> *"I tried out for the lead in* **Streetcar** *Named Desire. I didn't get the part. Those idiots don't know talent when they see it! I'm quitting. They're a rude bunch."*

Some years went by before Evelyn made another entry in the diary.

> *"I'm pregnant again! I blame Mike for this. It's his fault I wasn't protected right. Damn him! I don't want to go*

through all that again. I know he wants another child. He plotted against me. I hate this."

It seemed that Evelyn's diary entries followed a pattern. She only commented in it when something happened in her life she wanted to complain about. The next entry didn't come until two years later.

"Hello, diary, it's been a while. I've been really busy with Evie and Jean. Mike made certain I have help with the girls. I told him how much I suffer taking care of them and the house. He calls me moody but says he understands. It's all so boring and humdrum. Sometimes I feel like a prisoner. I need some excitement in my life. I've finally gotten my figure back. Carol's doing a nice job with my hair. I have some ideas for making my life more fun."

Another entry came almost a year after that.

"M. and I have something going. I love the naughtiness of it. I think something good will come of it. Time will tell. At least my life has become exciting."

Kim was too tired to continue reading. She went to sleep with the question still in her mind: Who was M?

In the morning she went back to the diary, speculating on "M." Drew Mitchell was often referred to as Mitch. He could be "M." Kim flipped all the way back to Evelyn's high school entries.

After Mike went into the service, Evelyn mentioned dating a number of other boys. There were references to Drew as well as to Thomas Ryan, but no one she referred to as "M."

Kim glanced at her watch and realized it was time to leave for work. Should she take the diary with her and continue reading at lunch? Not a good idea. For all she knew, this diary could provide leads to Evelyn's killer. She should keep it safe. Somewhere safer than under a sofa cushion.

Kim bit her lower lip, thinking. Her apartment was so tiny. She chose a spot under a shoe box in the back of her closet. If anyone searched her apartment, it wasn't a likely place to look—at least she hoped not.

Bert St. Croix plopped Evie's computer on top of Drew Mitchell's desk. He jumped back.

"Did I make you nervous?"

"Sheesh, give a person some warning!"

"You wanted the Gardner's laptop. Now you got it."

"If you erased anything you're in trouble." Mitchell stood, straightening.

"The only thing of value is a couple of emails threatening Evelyn. You're the one who might decide to do the erasing. But I've made copies."

"You accusing me of something?"

"Just letting you know."

"I'm taking this down to the tech lab. Top priority."

"Yeah, you do that."

Mitchell grabbed the laptop and took off. Bert watched him go with a small sense of satisfaction.

"Croix!" Nash's voice hit her ears. What now?

She pivoted. "Hi, Captain."

"You got anything on that string of burglaries?"

"I'm working on it," she said.

"Well, work a little faster. There's just been another one. Same M.O."

Bert sighed. "They hit during the day when the parents were at work and the kids at school?"

"You got it."

"Same development?"

"Ditto."

"Think I'll set up a map of the radius. It seems to me someone local is casing the houses, spotting the ones that are empty during the day. I'm probably looking for a perp who's either a housewife or a teenager, maybe one that lives in the development."

"Good thinking. Get on it."

Chapter Forty-Eight

"This'll have to be a short visit. What did you find out?" Bert didn't mean to pressure Kim, but she knew Kim was as eager for answers as she was. "Anything else of value in Evelyn's diary?"

"I haven't finished reading. I know she was a self-centered woman who didn't really love her children or her husband."

"So tell me something we didn't already know."

They'd met in front of the commons area and begun walking down College Avenue toward the park. Bert power-walked on long legs while Kim hurried to keep up.

"So anything useful?"

A gust of wind blew, and Kim pulled up the collar of her navy wool coat. "There were hints of flirting with Thomas Ryan and Drew Mitchell when Evie was still small. But nothing specific. Then she said she had 'something going with M.'"

"So who is 'M'? Drew Mitchell?"

"I thought about that. Elsewhere she refers to him as Drew."

"Maybe she was thinking differently about him once she thought of screwing with the guy."

"A possibility, I guess. This was a later entry."

"But you're not convinced."

"There isn't enough to go on. When I get back to the apartment, I'll pick up on the reading."

"Okay. I'll be on a burglary case all afternoon. You keep reading. Speed reading would be better." Bert looked around and said, "Nice park."

"You should come here with Fred Lincoln," Kim said.

Bert threw her a hard look. "What's that supposed to mean?"

"I just thought there was maybe something going on between you and him."

"Not really." Bert's eyes were fixed ahead of her.

"It could be good for both of you."

"Don't try to match make, okay?"

Definitely something there, Kim thought. "Time for me to go back to work. None of my business anyway."

"That's right. And don't smile that way."

That evening, Kim returned to the unpleasant task of reading Evelyn's Gardner's diary. She felt like a voyeur. Sitting cross-legged on the sofa, she found nothing more in the first few pages about "M." But about a year later:

> *"Thomas and I connected at the Christmas party Carol and Bob threw this year. Laura really watches him closely, but she loosened up after a few drinks. That gave Thom and me a chance to reminisce. Mike was called away on an emergency in the middle of the party. Typical!*
>
> *"Thom offered to drive me home. Laura looked like she'd swallowed a cow, but Thom prevailed. Laura drank too much and passed out in the car. Thom laid her across the backseat. Thom and I were cool with that. He had his hand on my knee and then he squeezed my breast as we drove along. Now that he knows where my house is, he can come over and we can get it on. Tonight was the best night I've had in a long time. I like being admired by men. I like flirting. Takes the edge off a boring existence. It's nice to know I've still got it."*

There was no question now in Kim's mind that Evelyn had decided to cheat on Mike long before she left him and the girls. Kim shook her head. The woman had little in the way of scruples or decency. But how much of that had been caused by sexual abuse in her youth? Didn't girls who were abused tend to have low self-esteem, and value themselves in relation to how much they were desired by men?

Growing up with Carl Reyner, her so-called father, had contributed to Kim's own lack of self-worth. Carl had been cold, critical and distant. Ma made excuses for the man. She claimed he'd been different before he was sent overseas and injured. Kim supposed that was true, but she could never forget how cruel he'd been to her. Worst of all, he'd murdered three innocent people at the V.A. hospital before turning the gun on himself and committing suicide. Kim shuddered at the memory.

She forced herself to continue reading. Now there were specifics about one of Evelyn's affairs. Fooling around with Bob Dodd hadn't been just a one-time thing. Did Carol Dodd know that her husband had lied to her? Either of the Dodds might have murdered Evelyn — Carol for revenge, Bob for silence.

Kim sighed. She didn't know any more than she had, and she hadn't narrowed the list of suspects.

Mayor Thomas Ryan, Mrs. Ryan, Evelyn's father, possibly her sister (Kim thought that would be a stretch), and neither last nor least Detective Mitchell: all had motives.

Chapter Forty-Nine

"So Mrs. Higgins, please give me the details regarding the burglary."

The middle-aged woman stared at Bert through thick lenses. "I already told the uniformed officer who answered my call, gave him all the details."

"That's true, ma'am, but I'm a detective and there have been similar robberies in your development. In fact, there's been quite a few of them. I'm examining them as a whole, looking for a pattern."

The woman smiled. "Oh, I see. This is like Sherlock Holmes."

"Maybe we can do some investigating together."

"You and me?" Mrs. Higgins looked both pleased and surprised.

"Sure, why not."

"Why don't you come in? It's so cold outside."

As Bert entered the living room, Mrs. Higgins said, "They took everything of value. Picked me clean. I feel violated."

"A normal reaction," Bert said, her tone of voice sympathetic.

Mrs. Higgins removed her glasses and rubbed her nose. "Since Charley passed on last year, I've been living in this house alone. It's not bad during the day because I go to work. But it's lonely here in the evenings. Every time there's a creak or the house settles, I jump. It'll be worse for me now. I'd sell in a minute if the price for houses wasn't so low in the area."

"I understand. You said the thieves got in by breaking the window glass at the rear of the house?"

"That's right. At first, I didn't even know I'd been robbed. But then I saw the TV was missing in the living room. Charley loved that wide screen. It was his pride and joy. He'd watch the Giants and the Jets during football season and I'd pop corn for him." There were tears in her eyes.

Bert nodded. "Mrs. Higgins, I noticed from our reports that the house next door to you hasn't been burglarized."

Mrs. Higgins blinked. "That's the Angelo house. And you're right. They've never been robbed."

"But the home on the other side of the Angelos has been burglarized."

"Yes, the Meyers house. They went and installed a burglar alarm. I'm going to do the same thing, although right now there's nothing left worth stealing. They took my jewelry, the computer and of course the TV, plus whatever cash I had."

"I take it no one was at home at the Meyers house at the time of their robbery."

Mrs. Higgins shook her head. "They were both at work."

"According to my reports, they were robbed during the day."

"Is that important?"

"There seems to be a pattern."

"Why don't you sit down? Can I fix you a cup of tea?"

"Thanks but I won't be staying long."

"Are you sure? It wouldn't be much trouble."

"Could you tell me about the Angelos? Is anyone home there during the day?"

"Certainly, Sandy's a stay-at-home mom. The Angelos have three small children. Sandy's mother comes over to help with babysitting. There's even a dog, a very noisy one."

"So there's usually someone home there every day?"

Mrs. Higgins nodded.

"Thank you," Bert said.

The woman looked surprised. "Is that all?"

"For now. You've been a big help."

As Bert walked across the grass to the Angelo house, she studied the neighborhood. This was not the wealthy part of Webster

Township. The houses were at least forty years old. Would a pro burglar choose a crime spree in this working class part of town over the lake area where the well-to-do lived? No way. The thieves had to be local. She'd bet her paycheck on that.

Bert rang the doorbell at the Angelo house. She heard a dog begin to bark and a child call out. A few minutes later, a woman cautiously opened the door a crack. She was young and looked frazzled.

"I'm not buying anything," she said. "If you're from those religious people, I don't want to be converted either."

"I haven't come to proselytize," Bert assured her. "I'm a police detective investigating the recent string of burglaries in your area." She showed her badge. "May I have a few minutes of your time?"

"Well, yes, sure. Come in." Mrs. Angelo led her into a living room crowded with toys. Three small children were playing, two girls and a boy.

"Everything's a mess."

"No problem. It has to be hard managing with little kids." Bert cleared a chair of dolls and sat down. Mrs. Angelo did the same.

"Mrs. Higgins told me that you haven't been robbed, but both her house and the one on the other side of yours have been."

"I guess we've been lucky. I've started locking my door when the kids aren't in the yard playing."

"Since you're home most of the time, I wonder if you might have seen anybody suspicious lurking around."

Mrs. Angelo raised her eyebrows. "Suspicious? I don't think so."

"Okay, let me put it another way. Has there been *anybody* hanging around?"

"Just some local kids, teenagers playing hooky. You know how kids are. They cut classes if they think they can get away with it."

"Did you happen to recognize them?"

Mrs. Angelo frowned. "I recognized one of the boys. There were three of them. The one I sort of know lives just up the block."

"Do you recall his name?"

"No, we're not friendly with the family. But I could point out the house to you. I always take walks with the children when the weather is nice. That boy would be hanging out drinking beer. I knew they were underage, and I remember thinking how the parents weren't doing their job."

"Will you show me which house?"

Mrs. Angelo turned to the older girl. "Nancy, keep an eye on your brother and sister for a moment. Don't let Kip put anything small in his mouth."

The little girl gave a solemn nod.

"Nancy's in kindergarten. She's very responsible," Mrs. Angelo said.

Bert followed the woman out the front door to the sidewalk.

"See that white house with the black shutters on the corner across the street? That's where the boy lives. I hope it helps. I feel especially bad for Mrs. Higgins. She's a nice old gal."

As Bert walked up the block, she flipped open her cell phone and called for backup.

Chapter Fifty

Driving home from work that evening, Kim thought a black car was following her. Had Drew Mitchell assigned an officer to follow her? Was he still thinking of charging her as a co-conspirator in Evelyn's murder?

When she sat down on her sofa to resume reading Evelyn's diary, she had to force herself to go ahead.

> "I feel as though I've been waiting my whole life for this. M. and I are great together. Some might think our meetings in motel rooms out of town are sleazy. But who cares about being ordinary? I am tired of the boring existence I lead. Tired of being a housewife and mother. I need more in my life. M. is so exciting. We don't talk about Mike when we're together. We don't discuss his wife either. The outside world does not exist for us. It's just M. and me. I don't care that he's older. He's definitely more experienced than I am. He's what I need."

The next entry was a month later.

> "M. likes his sex kinky which is fine with me. He handcuffed me to the bedpost spread eagled and entered me from the rear. Things got kind of scary but it was hot. Afterwards, I told him I wanted to leave Mike. I wanted him to divorce his wife and come live with me. M. surprised me by getting angry. He hit me, told me he wasn't leaving his wife and that I better never tell anyone about us or I'd be sorry."

Kim felt sick to her stomach. Clearly M. was a viable suspect. There was an entry a week after that.

> "M. called and asked me to meet him. Another motel room. The sex wasn't as good as usual. Too rough. Afterwards, M. surprised me. He handed me a lot of money. I got angry, told him I wasn't a hooker. I didn't want his cash, only him. He said the money was for me to get out of town and never come back. He said if I told anyone about us, especially Mike, I was dead. He pulled out a gun and pointed it at me. There was a lethal look in his eyes. I could see him as a stone cold killer.
>
> "I was furious. I told him I wasn't leaving my husband and children just because he was threatening me. He hit me really hard, knocked the wind out of me and made more threats. I got scared.
>
> "The money had fallen on the floor. I managed to pick it up and place it in my purse. Then I got dressed. All the time I was trying to think straight and I couldn't. What was I going to do?"

The next entry, the last in the diary, was brief:

> "I told Mike I was leaving him. It was the hardest thing I ever had to do. But I believe M. would have murdered me if I didn't. I made up a story about another man and how we were going off to Hollywood so I could pursue an acting career. I cleaned out the joint bank account so I'll have that money as well as what M. gave me. Mike is devastated. The girls don't understand. I hate the way they looked at me. They're both so young. I can't explain it to them. Maybe some day I'll come back. Maybe not. I guess I will get my shot at being an actress after all."

That was the end. The rest of the pages were blank. Kim glanced through them carefully just to be sure, but there was nothing more. God, how awful. She felt a deep sense of sadness. She hadn't liked the woman, but after reading the diary she felt sympathy for Evelyn. Mike's wife had clearly needed psychotherapy. She should have confided in Mike, should have turned to him for help and support. Instead she had hidden her emotional problems.

She had been a better actress than anyone knew.

So who was "M"? The man was older, married, and predatory. Evelyn had slept with him. He was hard, ruthless and threatened to kill. When Evelyn had come back, had "M" carried out his threat?

Kim sat and stared at the diary. She had a suspicion who the mystery lover was. If she was right, it all fit together. But confronting "M" was going to be dangerous. She dialed Bert's cell.

Chapter Fifty-One

"I'm setting up a six-pack," Bert said.

"What's that?" Kim asked. She was certain Bert wasn't talking about beer.

"It's a set of six pictures. I'm going to show them to April. Ask her if she can pick out the older man she saw with Evelyn at the Galaxy Lounge. So we'll meet at the Galaxy after work tomorrow?"

Kim agreed. "I tried to phone you earlier but all I got was your message pickup."

"I was finishing up on a burglary case. Busy all day with it. Finally found out who was behind the thefts."

"Who was it?"

"Would you believe a housewife? Mother of two teenage boys, a single mom. She was the brains of the operation. Ran the whole burglary ring from her house. The place is full of stolen goods. The boys would case the houses in the area, find out who worked and who didn't. Piece of cake breaking in from the rear, especially the houses that faced the woods where no neighbors would be watching. The mother was shrewd. She taught the boys just what to take, mostly money and jewelry."

"Congratulations on breaking the case," Kim said.

"It's not a big bust, but at least people will be getting some of their valuables back after the case ends."

"I suppose it's a sure conviction."

"Someone like Fred Lincoln will defend them. I can see him pleading that the housewife was a single parent desperate for money, trying to prevent foreclosure of her home. Mark my words. The case will be plea-bargained."

Kim didn't doubt it. She went to sleep that night dreaming of burglars breaking back windows, and then the dreams shifted to Evelyn Gardner handcuffed to a bedpost.

Kim gazed at the ceiling of the Galaxy Lounge and felt as if she were visiting a planetarium. "Waiting long?" Bert slid into the seat opposite her.

"Just a few minutes."

"You chose a good table," Bert said. "This booth has privacy."

Kim studied her friend. Bert was wearing a man-tailored brown suit with a gold turtleneck. She appeared both professional and classy. Kim assumed Bert had come directly from work as she had. They both looked like business women meeting for a cocktail—if the telling bulge of Bert's holstered weapon beneath her jacket was ignored.

"I spoke to April. She'll be able to take a break and join us in a few minutes," Kim said.

As if on cue, April came to their table. "Give me your drink order first," she said. "Frank's in one of his shitty moods, then again when isn't he?"

"I don't want to get you in any trouble," Bert said, "but this is important."

"I got that idea." April took their order and left.

Bert pulled out a grouping of six photos from a carrying bag. She also placed a photo of Evelyn Gardner on the table. "Okay, let's hope she can I.D. him for us."

Kim frowned. "You really think she can? I doubt I'd be able to do it."

"We'll see."

April returned with the drinks, cranberry juice with a twist of lime for Bert, orange juice for Kim.

"What, no peanuts? Don't we rate anymore?" Bert said.

April was abashed. "I'll get them."

"Don't bother. I was only joking."

"Hard to know when you're kidding since you do it so seldom," April said.

"She's got a point," Kim agreed.

"That's right, beat up on the cop."

"Poor you," April said.

Bert cleared her throat. "Back to the reason we're here. April, remember we showed you a picture of this woman?"

April sat down and stared at Evelyn's photo. "Sure. I told you I saw her with Mayor Ryan."

"Right. You also mentioned you saw her another time with an older man. Can you possibly recall what that man looked like?"

"I don't know." April raised her eyebrows.

"I want you to look at some pictures. See if any of these men look familiar. See if one of them was the one you saw with Evelyn Gardner."

April Nevins studied each of the photos. She looked up. "I'm fairly certain it was this one right here." She tapped with a painted fingernail.

"You're sure?" Bert said.

"Hey, it was a while back. I see a lot of people. But I did notice them. She looked unhappy, nervous. He looked angry. I wondered about that. I remember thinking they wouldn't leave a tip. So I did kind of keep an eye on them. The older guy looked like someone you wouldn't want to mess with. He a gangster or something?"

"Or something." Bert exchanged a look with Kim.

"You want to tell me if I identified the person you're targeting?"

"For right now, April, I kind of think it's best if you don't know too much."

April turned from Bert to Kim. "What's going on?"

"We'll be in touch," Bert said. "Don't discuss this with anyone."

"Have it your way." April flounced off.

"You could have told her," Kim said.

"Best not. She just identified Sam Morgan, Webster Township's Chief of Police. as being here in the company of the murder vic shortly before she died. I don't want to put April in any more danger than necessary."

"What about you?" Kim said.

"I can take care of myself."

"So 'M' is Chief Morgan."

"Makes sense. Evelyn would have met him at some cop social function, maybe flirted with him. He took it from there."

"He threatened her. Told her she had to leave town or he'd kill her. He gave her money so she would go. Evelyn made up that whole story about leaving Mike for another man."

"Don't feel too sorry for the woman."

"Evelyn didn't deserve to be murdered. You think Morgan killed her?"

Bert stared at her drink. "I think it's a real possibility. It would explain why Drew Mitchell is so determined to stick Mike for Evelyn's murder. He's Morgan's flunky. Whatever the chief tells him to do, he does it, including blowing up the mayor's car. Can I prove it? No. But I'm pretty sure."

"So you do think Morgan is guilty of murdering Evelyn and her friend Rick Jameson?"

Bert shrugged. "One thing kind of makes me wonder. Morgan's been a widower for a few years now. The affair with Evelyn would be old news. Since he's got no wife to protect, why worry? I mean a guy with his ego, he's used to being attacked for being corrupt and never seems to care. Why would this bother him?"

"Maybe Evelyn knew something more incriminating about him."

"She did know him intimately. I don't think the chief would permit anyone to blackmail him."

"He'd already threatened to kill her," Kim said. "We have to tell Fred Lincoln about this."

"Right." Bert flipped open her cell phone. "I'll take care of that right now."

Chapter Fifty-Two

"Go home," Bert said. There were shadows of fatigue under Kim's eyes. "I'll have a word with Lincoln and get back to you if anything new comes up."

Bert got Fred Lincoln's machine and left a message. After Kim left, she kicked back and enjoyed her juice. Things were looking up, if she didn't think about the job of taking down the police chief. April came by with a bowl of peanuts.

"Want another juice?"

"No, I'm good."

"Did I help you?"

She eyeballed April. "You did."

"Good." April smiled. "You and Lieutenant Gardner saved my life. I haven't forgotten. I owe you both."

"April, we were doing our jobs. You don't owe us anything."

"Yeah, I do. You went the extra mile for me. Especially you. I was all screwed up. You helped me get it together. So any way I can help in my own small way, I will." With that, April went on to take an order at a nearby table.

Bert's cell rang and she flipped it open it to find that Fred Lincoln was calling her back.

"Got something interesting to tell you that I think will help Lieutenant Gardner."

"Great. I'm finishing for the day. Why don't we meet for dinner?"

Bert hesitated. "I don't really want to talk about this in a public place."

"Then I've got the perfect location for us. Can't get more private. Want me to pick you up?"

"Is it in New Brunswick?"

"It is."

"I'll meet you. Give me the address." Bert removed her ballpoint and small black notebook from her bag and took down the information. She studied the address he gave her.

"Your apartment?"

"You got it right, detective."

She shifted in her chair. "I don't think that's such a great idea."

"Happens I'm a real good cook. We both need to eat. Promise to behave myself."

"If you don't, I might have to hurt you."

"Ouch! Just dinner and conversation. Okay? You call the shots, sexy lady."

"Half an hour," she said.

What the hell. Fred Lincoln didn't know it yet, but he just might get lucky tonight.

Kim fell into a deep, exhausted sleep that night. Sometime after midnight, she began to dream. She floated into Mike's cell and sat down beside him on his bunk. But he was asleep and didn't seem to be aware that she had joined him. Dare she wake him? Something made her think it was important that they communicate.

"Mike, wake up." He didn't move. She called his name again but got no response. She tried to shake him. He still didn't budge. It was then that she looked down at her body and noticed her transparency. Kim cried out. Mike moved in his sleep but still did not awaken.

"This isn't real," she said to herself. "I'm not with Mike. I'm having a dream." But even as she said it, Kim felt a sense of wrongness surrounding her.

Kim turned when she heard the cell opening. Two large corrections officers walked in. They grabbed Mike and shook him. Mike was quickly alert.

"What do you want?"

"You," the bigger of the two guards said.

"What for? It's the middle of the night."

"Don't worry about it." With that, he ripped off Mike's shirt and wound it around one ham sized fist. "Hold him down," the guard said to his companion.

Mike fought the guards. Kim screamed but no one heard her. The larger guard roped the shirt around Mike's neck and began tightening it like a noose. It was two against one. Kim tried to aid Mike against their brute force. But she was nothing more than an insubstantial ghost. She continued to scream and wouldn't stop. "You're killing him!"

"We're going to make it look like you hung yourself," the larger guard said to Mike. "Stop fighting it! That's what I was told to do. A cop who murdered his wife should commit suicide. Saves the state the cost of a trial."

"Stop!" Kim yelled. Still neither the guards nor Mike appeared to hear her.

Kim heard banging. There were loud smashing noises. Were they coming to rescue Mike?

A voice cried, "What's going on? Kim can you hear me? Do you need help? Should we call the police?"

Kim was confused, disoriented. She opened her eyes and found herself lying on the sofa bed. What had happened? She must have been dreaming. But she'd never had a dream that seemed so real and vivid in her life. And then she realized what it must mean. She'd had a vision, been given a premonition.

The pounding at her door continued. "Kim, what's going on?"

She managed to drag herself to her feet, feeling for the lamp switch on the end table.

Staggering to the door, Kim threw it open. The two graduate students who were her upstairs neighbors stared at her.

"Thank God. Are you okay? Su was ready to call the cops," Jessica said as she bustled into the apartment. "We heard you screaming and were afraid someone was raping or murdering you."

"Are you all right?" Su demanded.

"It was just a dream, a terrible nightmare," Kim said.

Jessica held a golf club double-handed, ready for use as a

weapon. She prowled the apartment scowling, ready to pounce on any intruder. Finally she lowered the club. "You got some pair of lungs."

"Sorry," Kim said. "I'm really sorry. Please go back to sleep."

"If you are all right," Su said.

"Thank you both for checking on me."

Kim was relieved when her neighbors closed the door and she heard them climb the steps back to their own apartment. She knew she hadn't been dreaming. It was a vision, a premonition, just as Joseph's dream in the Bible had been both a prophecy and a warning. Mike was going to be murdered. She was certain it hadn't happened yet, but it would if she didn't act soon.

Kim located her cell phone and pressed Bert's number. The phone rang a number of times before Bert said, "Hell, Kim this better be important." Bert's voice was thick with sleep.

"I had to wake you. They're going to kill Mike in his cell if we don't act fast."

"What are you talking about? How do you know?"

"I saw it happening. I had a vision."

"Oh, crap. You sure it wasn't just some nightmare?"

"You have to believe me. It wasn't a normal dream. We've got to help him. Please use whatever contacts you have."

"Hold on."

Kim waited. She could hear a muffled conversation. Then a pause as if Bert walked to another room.

"Okay, I'm here with Fred Lincoln—don't ask any questions. I told him I had a tip that Mike was going to be attacked in his cell tonight. He says it's impossible. Security's tight. No way it could happen. Does that relieve your mind?"

"No. Put him on the phone."

Bert sighed, and a moment later Fred Lincoln came on. "Ms. Reynolds? I have as much regard for my client as you do. Believe me, he's in maximum security. No one's getting to him."

"The guards can and will," Kim said. "Please, Mr. Lincoln, he needs your help right now. This can't wait."

There was a brief silence. "You're certain?"

"I've never been more certain of anything in my life."

"All right. There's a judge I'm friends with. He's got a lot of juice. I'll wake him. He'll get me inside."

"I'll go with you," Bert said as she snatched the phone back. "Sit tight, Kim. We'll let you know what happens."

Chapter Fifty-Three

Michael Gardner dreamt of Kim Reynolds. In the dream she sat beside him in the jail cell.

"I love you so much," she said.

"I didn't think I'd see you again."

"I know."

"Are you all right?" He tried to caress her but Kim felt insubstantial as air.

"I've come to warn you," she said. "I had a vision. They're coming to kill you tonight. I need to protect you."

Gardner reached out to her again, but she disappeared. He felt bereft.

The sound of the cell grinding open woke him with a start. He opened his eyes and stared up at the two corrections officers.

"What are you doing here?"

"We're going to help you make amends for what you done to your wife. We know how bad your conscience must be hurting." Gardner recognized the two correction officers as the ones who'd taken him to the showers where he'd nearly been killed. He recalled his dream and Kim's warning. His heart beat faster.

"Hand over your shirt," the older of the two guards said. He was a big man with a large gut who wore a mustache that emphasized his long nose.

"My shirt? What for?"

The younger and leaner of the two gave him a hard shove. "Just do what Sarge says."

Gardner didn't respond or move.

"J.D., this one won't cooperate," the older guard said.

The younger man drew a baton from his pocket, flicked his wrist. Gardner jumped to his feet. When the attack came, it was quick and smooth. But Gardner was already in motion, sidestepping the baton, slamming the older guard into the attacker, and then closing in on the pair. He had feet, knees and fists, and he used them all.

Kim sat staring at her phone. When it finally rang, she grabbed it.

"Kim, you were right," Bert said. "It's okay. We got there in time."

She sat down heavily. "Thank God."

"They had a towel sort of twisted around his neck. The warden himself put a stop to everything."

"Mike's really all right?" She reminded herself to breathe.

"A doctor's looking at him, but he seemed okay. The guards got pretty roughed up." Bert chuckled. "No telling who would have won that one. Mike said something funny."

"What's that?"

"He said you warned him."

Kim felt light-headed. "They were supposed to use his shirt," she said. "To hang him."

"Mike's shirt's still on his back. You saved him twice."

"Do we know who's responsible?"

"The guards aren't talking, but I have a damn good idea."

"So do I," Kim said. "What are we going to do about it?"

Chapter Fifty-Four

Bert said to Kim, "I do the talking. Agreed?"

Kim gave a short nod. It was ten a.m. The two of them stood a few steps from the door to Chief Sam Morgan's office.

"Okay, I guess we're ready then." Bert opened the door.

Morgan looked up from his desk. He ignored Kim and said to Bert, "You should have made an appointment, detective."

"This won't take long."

"I have a meeting to attend." Morgan looked down at his watch.

"I want to talk to you about Mike and Evelyn Gardner," Bert said. "And about two jailhouse guards who tried last night to murder Mike."

"Murder Gardner?" Sam Morgan glared at her. "I have no idea what you're talking about."

"I think those two corrections officers will talk even if you don't. It will mean the end of your career. Maybe you should think of resigning. Good time of the year to get out of the cold. The Caribbean's nice."

Morgan stood up, rapped a clenched fist on his desk. "Detective—get out of my office!"

Bert didn't move. "We have evidence," she said, "a diary written by Evelyn Gardner telling about her sordid affair with you in her own words."

Morgan's face reddened. "Are you trying to blackmail me? I'll tell you right now I won't stand for it."

"We're not after blackmail money like Evelyn. We believe you murdered her as well as her boyfriend and that you set Mike Gardner up to take the fall."

Morgan looked ready to explode. "Do you have any clue what

you're saying and who you're saying it to? You work for me! And your badge depends on my conviction that you're not a complete idiot—which I now doubt. Gardner murdered his wife."

Kim felt a shock. She had the distinct impression the chief believed what he said. She spoke up. "It appears I know Mike much better than you do."

"I'm sure that's true," Morgan said. "And beside the point."

She tried again. "I know that Michael Gardner isn't guilty of killing Evelyn. There are a number of people she was trying to blackmail including you who had reason to kill her."

"You're a person of interest to say the least," Bert said.

Morgan ignored Bert, staring at Kim. "I can prove my whereabouts at the time of Mrs. Gardner's death, which is more than can be said for your boyfriend, Ms. Reynolds."

"If that diary gets turned over to Mike's attorney, you're going to look dirty," Bert said.

"I don't like people who threaten me, detective."

Bert stood firm. "I don't like people who threaten me either. And I don't like killers. Whether you murdered Evelyn or not, you arranged for Mike to be killed. You're lucky we managed to stop it in time."

He shook his head. "This is getting old. You barge in here like some bad-movie cop, accuse me of murder and attempted murder . . . me, the god-damned chief of police. For evidence? You've got dirty stories in a diary. If you know anything about Evelyn, you know she covered a lot of ground. Even you, Ms. Reynolds, seem aware of that. If I tried to murder everyone who threatened me—" He threw up his hands. "I know you two are fond of Mike Gardner. If the evidence weren't against him, I'd be on your side."

"Drew Mitchell is cooking the case," Bert snapped. "I assume on your orders."

"Have I ever ordered anyone on this force to 'cook a case'? Anyone you know of? Ever?" He waved a hand. "Even if I were that kind of cop, who would go along with it? You? Gardner?

Mitchell? Much as you hate Mitch, have you ever seen him railroad anyone?"

"He's doing it now. And, Chief Morgan, somebody who could reach into the jail tried to have Mike murdered last night."

"Do you have any evidence of *that*?"

"The warden arrived during the attack. Mike's lawyer and I were there."

Morgan picked up his phone. "Effie? Find out what happened with Mike Gardner at the jail last night. There should be a report." He slammed down the phone. He looked at Bert with distaste. "Okay, detective. I can see how this looks to you. Personally, I'm tempted to fire your ass on the spot. But—"

"But there's the diary?"

"That doesn't scare me." He gave a nasty smile. "Might even get me some action around town. No, it's a practical but. You and Detective Mitchell are about all I've got. You want to chase leads, get on it. I'll send word down that you're on the case. I hope you do better than you've done so far."

"I'm still not sure about you," Bert said.

"Nor I about you, Detective St. Croix." As they headed for the door, he called after them. "Did Evelyn say anything good about me in that diary?"

They made it out to the parking lot before either of them spoke.

"I really walked into it," Bert said. "The bastard's right. I don't have evidence."

"But you're on the case," Kim pointed out.

"So I am. Until I get taken off."

"Do you think Morgan killed Evelyn?"

Bert exchanged a look with her. "I don't know. I don't feel so confident."

"Bert, I don't think he did. He's capable, no doubt about that. But my intuition tells me he was telling us the truth—at least about

Evelyn. If he really believed Mike murdered Evelyn, he might have felt justified in having Mike killed in jail."

"No mess left around to implicate him," Bert said. "No worry about what might have come out in a trial."

"He could have done one thing but not the other. Which still means he's a monster."

"And dangerous," Bert said. "Thanks for that thought."

Chapter Fifty-Five

Bert watched her friend drive off. She hoped Kim would try to catch up on her sleep; she looked exhausted. As for herself, although she'd only had a few hours sleep, she felt stoked—and only a little chastened by the fiasco with Chief Morgan.

She had a busy day ahead.

At the Clip Joint, Bert asked the girl sweeping up which one of the beauticians was Carol Dodd. The girl pointed to a platinum blonde wearing bright red lipstick with matching blood red fingernails. Bert walked over to her as the hairdresser put the finishing touches on an elderly woman's champagne curls.

"You Carol Dodd?"

"That's me." Carol surveyed Bert's ebony braids with a critical eye. "Sweetie, I don't do black gals, not so great with extensions, but I can send you to someone who'll do a good job with your kind of hair."

"I'm a detective with the Webster Township P.D." Bert flashed her badge. "I'm here to talk to you about Evelyn Gardner."

The old woman got out of the chair gingerly, thanked Carol and tottered off.

Carol's expression hardened. "I've had nothing whatever to do with Evelyn since I found the bitch in bed with my husband. I don't know anything about her death. If her husband killed her, I sympathize with him. Now would you please leave my shop?"

"I'd love to, but I can't. I need to know exactly what you were doing during the hours that Evelyn was killed."

"Can't that wait? I have customers now. This is bad for business."

"We can do it here and now or down at police headquarters. That would be even worse for business. It's your call."

"All right," said Carol Dodd.

Kim took a long nap that afternoon and woke up feeling better. There had been no dreams or visions. For that alone she was grateful.

She caught sight of Evelyn's diary on the kitchen counter. She called Bert's cell and asked if she should drop the book at police headquarters.

"I definitely want it," Bert said. "The diary needs to be locked up in a safe place. I'm not at headquarters. I'm in the field. Tell you what, I'll come by later and get it."

'How about coming for dinner? I can cook."

"Don't go to the trouble. I'll pick up pizza or Chinese take-out. Let's celebrate."

When Bert arrived, Kim set the pizza in the oven to warm and opened a bottle of Chianti. She asked Bert, "What did Fred Lincoln think when you told him why I phoned?"

Bert lowered her eyes. "I didn't exactly tell him the truth."

"Why not?"

"It's like this. If I told him that you have psychic ability and saw that Mike was about to be attacked in jail, he would have thought you were psycho not psychic. So what I said was that an informant had called you with a tip, that this informant was totally reliable, someone who owed Mike Gardner a favor but didn't want to talk directly to the cops. Fred grunted but believed me and got moving quick."

"It was lucky for Mike that the two of you were spending the night together. By the way I think that's wonderful."

Bert's color deepened. "Don't make too much of that. It was a momentary weakness on my part. I don't intend for it to become a habit."

"Mr. Lincoln is a very nice man. Anyone can see that. I believe you and he would make a wonderful couple."

"We'll see," Bert said with an uneasy shrug. "And don't ask me if he's good in bed."

"Wouldn't dream of it." Kim couldn't help smiling. "But is he?"

"Not bad."

They drank their wine and ate their pizza in companionable silence.

When they finished, Kim said, "So who did you interview today?"

"First Carol Dodd, then her husband."

Kim leaned forward in her chair. "And?"

"Not much to tell. They provided alibis for each other for part of the time. One or both of them could have killed Evelyn. Hard to tell."

"Which reminds me. Here's Evelyn's diary." Kim handed Bert the book.

"Pick up anything else from it? Any e.s.p. vibes?"

"I keep telling you, it doesn't work that way."

"Okay, just asking." Bert flipped through the diary, then glanced at the beginning and the end. She shook her head. "I just wish we could have found Evelyn's cell phone. Or Jameson's. At least I'm free to work on the case now."

Chapter Fifty-Six

At the library the next day, Kim went through the motions, her mind preoccupied with the murders. She wished she could help with the investigation. Bert was the professional. Bert had studied criminal justice at college. Bert had been a cop in New York City. So how could a mere reference librarian be of real help? And yet her instincts told her she could and should be part of the solution.

On her lunch break, Kim phoned Bert. "How's the investigation going?"

"From what I can tell, it's not likely that Evelyn's father or her sister were in town when she was murdered. Then again, I can't say for certain. Possibly Maryann drove in that day. But she claims to have been sick with the flu and had a doctor's appointment that morning, which I did verify. No flights out from Texas put Cooper here. I'll research that some more though."

"I have an idea, but I'd like to explain it to you in person."

"Okay, I'll meet you over at the Galaxy after work. That way I can keep April in the loop as well."

"Sounds like a plan," Kim agreed.

April was animated when Kim arrived. "Bert says you had a go at Sam Morgan. That must have been something!"

"It was something," Kim said dryly. She slid into the corner booth across from the detective. "I guess Bert told you we still don't know who murdered Mike's wife."

"Yeah," April said in disbelief. "I thought you had it licked. Cranberry juice for both of you?"

"Fine for me," Kim said.

Bert nodded. She waited until April left. "So what was your idea?"

"I know this is going to sound a little over the top. But suppose I let each of the suspects know that Evelyn kept a diary and tell them I found something in it that would prove embarrassing to them? Then I say that I want money to keep quiet. I'm willing to sell them the diary so there's no evidence. I'd call the exchange of money between us a sign of good faith."

Bert rested her chin on her hands. "So then the murderer comes out of the woodwork and tries to kill you?"

"And you of course catch that person in the act."

"Yeah, I think I saw that in the movies once or twice. Works well in fiction but not in real life. For one thing, who's going to be protecting you 24/7? We don't have that kind of police manpower. Sorry, that idea is as dangerous as it is dumb. No offense, but I expect better from you."

April set their drinks on the table. "Peanuts, pretzels or both?"

"Neither," Bert said.

"All right," April said. She looked from Bert to Kim with puzzlement and walked away.

"You were kind of rude to her, weren't you?" Kim said.

"There's more that needs saying. You got me ticked off. Your idea could get you killed. I can't believe someone as sensible as you would consider it for a second."

People arrived at a nearby table, chatting gaily, and Kim looked around.

"Mayor Ryan and his wife are looking prosperous," Bert said.

The well-dressed couple were smiling into each other's eyes. Thomas Ryan's beefy frame was stuffed into an expensive suit. Laura Berg Ryan removed a designer coat to reveal a matching dress in forest green silk. She wore a gold necklace studded with emeralds, diamonds and pearls. Twinkling at her ears were emerald and gold earrings. The earrings had a quieter, antique look that didn't match the gaudy necklace. Kim had to admit the woman looked striking. Her bright auburn hair appeared to have been recently colored and styled by a pro. Kim wondered if Carol Dodd was Laura Berg's hairdresser. Wouldn't that prove interesting?

She and Bert watched as Thomas Ryan called April over and ordered champagne.

"I wonder what they're celebrating," Bert said.

Mrs. Ryan noticed Bert and Kim watching her and her husband. She touched her husband's arm and whispered. He followed her glance.

"Waitress," Ryan called out. "We've changed our minds. Cancel our order. We're leaving."

April approached them. "Are you sure? Can I get you something else instead?"

Ryan looked over at Bert and Kim. "No, we have to go." He took out his wallet, pulled out a bill and handed it to April. Then he and his wife took off.

April came over to their table, hands on hips. "You two are scaring the customers away. What gives?"

Bert shrugged. "Guilty conscience maybe. I spoke to them this morning about Evelyn Gardner. They both assured me they hadn't seen her since she returned."

"I don't know about the woman with the mayor," April said.

"His wife," Bert responded.

"Whatever. But I did see him with Mrs. Gardner not that long ago. So that was a big, fat lie." April sounded indignant.

"People lie to cops all the time," Bert observed. "It's human nature."

April sniffed. "Hard to find an honest politician."

Chapter Fifty-Seven

When Kim arrived at her apartment, the land line was ringing. She caught the phone on the third ring and recognized Louise Gardner's voice. "Am I catching you at a bad time?"

"No, just coming in. How are you?"

"I'm good. The reason for the call is that tomorrow is Evie's birthday. It won't be a very happy one for her with her dad in jail. I was hoping you could come over to celebrate with us. It'll just be family."

"I'd love to be there. What should I bring?"

"Just yourself," Louise said.

"I'd like to buy something for Evie that she'd like. Can you think of anything?"

"I'm certain anything you bring will be fine."

Kim sat down trying to think what a fifteen-year-old girl might like to get as a gift. Perfume? Jewelry? She had no idea what Evie's tastes were. She decided to pick up a gift certificate at one of the department stores in the mall after work the next day.

The promised snow was holding off the next evening, and Kim had a positive feeling that this would turn out to be a good evening.

Jean greeted her at the door. "We're having a party for Evie 'cause it's her birthday," the child confided.

"I know. That's why I came."

Jean took her hand. "Come on, Kim. We're going to have ice cream cake and hot chocolate. Evie wanted the ice cream cake, 'cause Dad always says it's not a birthday unless we have one."

Kim smile. "Your dad is a very wise man."

Jean gave a solemn nod. "Do you think he can come home soon? I miss him a whole lot."

"Bert is working very hard to bring him back to you, honey." Kim reached down and hugged the young girl.

They entered the dining room where the family was seated around the table. Louise stood up and came toward her.

"You're right on time for dessert. There's plenty of leftovers in case you'd like me to fix you a dinner plate."

"No, I'm fine." She reached into her handbag and brought out the gift certificate. Then she turned to Evie who was looking grown-up this evening with make-up, a pretty dress and even some jewelry. "Evie, this is for you. Happy birthday."

Evie stood up from her place at the table, came forward and kissed Kim on the cheek. She accepted the proffered gift. "Thanks, Kim."

"You look lovely," Kim said.

"See my bracelet?"

Kim looked down. Evie wore a gold and emerald bracelet on her wrist. "Aunt Louise gave it to me. It belonged to Dad and Uncle Chuck's mother, my grandmother, and her mother before her."

"It's an antique then," Kim said, studying the bracelet. "It's beautiful."

"One of a kind piece," Louise said, "although there are earrings to match. When Chuck and Mike's mother passed away, she left the bracelet to me and the earrings to Evelyn."

"It would be nice to keep the two pieces together," Kim said.

She continued to study the bracelet. She didn't know very much about good jewelry, but this was distinctive. Louise called it a one of a kind piece. Kim believed that. Yet there was something familiar about the workmanship of the bracelet.

"I gather the earrings were made to match the bracelet?"

"Yes, they were," Louise said.

"Evelyn wore them a lot," Evie said. "She had pierced ears. Dad said I can get mine pierced when I'm sixteen."

Kim said, "Bert and I were in your house. We didn't see earrings to match your bracelet."

"Evelyn was wearing them the day she died," Evie said. "I remember her having the earrings on when I left for school that morning. Jean, didn't you ask her if she was going out because she looked so nice?"

Jean nodded her head. "Mom looked pretty. She said she was expecting company later."

Kim stared at Jean. "Did your mother happen to say who was coming over to visit?"

Jean shook her head.

"Are you sure?" Kim persisted.

Jean scrunched her face.

"Kim, I overheard the conversation," Evie said. "Evelyn didn't tell Jean anything else. Sorry. Do you think it might have been important?

"I do."

The boys began banging their plates. "Cake, cake we want ice cream cake," Jerry said.

"Not a birthday without ice cream cake," Evie said.

Kim couldn't stop thinking about the missing earrings. She excused herself as soon as the dessert was demolished.

"Do you have to leave so soon?" Louise asked. "I was hoping you'd stay for a while. We enjoy your company."

"That's good to hear," Kim said. "And I appreciate you including me in your family celebration. But there's something I need to check out. I promise to be in touch soon. Hopefully with some good news."

Kim was preoccupied on the drive back to Webster Township. Should she call Bert, tell her of the suspicion she had? No, first she should confirm the accuracy of her information.

The lights were still on at Ryan's Funeral Home when she drove into an almost empty parking lot. She hurried to the front entrance.

"We're closed," a male voice called out as she entered.

"Sorry, Mr. Ryan, but I need to see you and your wife for a few minutes."

She walked into a viewing room, where the Ryans were neatening the area.

"We're about to leave," Mrs. Ryan said. "The viewing is over for tonight."

"Yes, I understand, but I have a few questions that I hope you can help me answer."

The Ryans exchanged looks.

"What do you want to know?"

"It's about Evelyn Gardner."

Laura Ryan groaned. "Not that again. Why are you and that black detective bothering us?"

"When I saw you yesterday evening, it brought a question to mind."

"If you must know, we were out celebrating last night because we heard that Chief Morgan will be resigning." Her mouth was tight.

"You were wearing unusual earrings last night."

"So what?" Laura Ryan snapped.

"They looked like a pair of earrings Evelyn Gardner wore."

"I guess we had similar taste in jewelry. Probably we shopped at the same store."

"Really? Because I was told that Evelyn's earrings were one of a kind antiques. Where are your earrings now?"

"In my jewelry box. They match the necklace my darling Thom bought me as an anniversary present."

Mayor Ryan stepped closer to Kim. "Look here, I don't understand this. Why are you questioning my wife about earrings of all things? I am going to register a complaint about you for harassment."

Kim realized she wasn't getting very far. She was an amateur at interrogating, and now she had tipped off the Ryans about the earrings. They would likely get rid of the jewelry. She felt desperate.

Another tactic was called for.

"Forgive me," Kim said. "I apologize. It's just that Evelyn mentioned you both in her diary. There was certain information about you in it that makes you suspects in her murder."

"That's ridiculous," Laura said. "I don't believe you. Where's this diary? I want to see it."

"We can arrange that," Kim said evenly. "I'll phone you tomorrow."

She got out of the funeral home as fast as she could move. Mayor Ryan called after her but she ignored him.

After she drove back to her apartment, Kim phoned Bert. Her friend didn't answer and so she left an urgent message. She lay down on top of her sofa, pulling a blanket around her and waited. This would be one long night and she did not intend to sleep.

Chapter Fifty-Eight

She was so tired that she started to doze. Banging at the door woke her with a start. She glanced over at her clock radio and saw that it was only eleven p.m.

"Who's there?" she called out.

No answer. She went to the kitchen and reached for a sharp knife. Then her cell phone rang. She snatched it up and heard Bert's voice.

"Kim, what's going on? I just saw your message. I was at the jail. They let me talk with Mike. . . ."

"I have a good idea who killed Evelyn," Kim said. "That party is trying to get into my apartment right now. So if you could get here as soon as possible, I would appreciate—"

There was a rattling noise from the sliding glass door facing the courtyard. She set the phone on her countertop.

"Who's there?" she called out. "Show yourself."

"It's just me. I came to have a look at that diary you mentioned."

"Come around the front and I'll let you in," Kim called out to the figure at the back door.

Kim placed the knife behind her. She needed to stall for time. The banging resumed at the front door. Kim waited. The banging continued.

"Just a minute!" Kim called out.

"Hurry up, this is important."

Kim finally pulled open her door, allowing Laura Ryan to enter her tiny apartment. Laura stalked in, glanced around, and sniffed the air with distaste. Then she closed the door behind her.

Kim sized her up. "I hope you brought the earrings we talked about, the ones that look exactly like those Evelyn Gardner owned."

"As a matter of fact, I didn't."

"You didn't bring the earrings because you murdered Evelyn and then stole them from her corpse."

Their eyes met.

"What did Evelyn say about me in her diary?" Laura demanded.

Kim decided to improvise. "What do you think Evelyn wrote about you?"

"You don't know anything about me. You're lying. What could Evelyn possibly have written?"

"You mean about her meeting with your husband again, resuming their former affair and then blackmailing him?"

"That's a lie!"

Laura's face was red with anger, her eyes unnaturally bright.

"Evelyn would not have given you her earrings. They were a family heirloom, something she treasured."

"She sold them to me," Laura said.

Kim shook her head. "She was wearing those earrings when her daughters left for school the morning of the day she died. And she was expecting company. You were the person she was waiting for, weren't you? She was demanding money from you, wasn't she?"

"All right," Laura admitted, "I did find out that evil bitch was trying to blackmail Thom. He was foolish when it came to her. So stupid!"

"But he wasn't the one who murdered her, was he? A man wouldn't notice something like earrings—most men wouldn't. But you would."

"No, I don't suppose many men pay much attention to earrings." Laura reached into her coat pocket and removed a snub nose revolver.

Kim stared at it. "You'll wake my neighbors if you shoot me. They'll be down here in a flash. You won't get away with another murder."

"You don't think so? I've killed two blackmailing scum. I think I can manage one more troublemaker. Anyway, I don't plan to kill you here. We'll take a ride together. You just won't be returning." Laura smiled at the thought. "Before we go, get that diary."

"I don't think I will," Kim said. "Why don't we just talk about Richard Jameson? How did he know you killed Evelyn?"

"He didn't. Evelyn told him about planning to meet me, how I was going to pay her off. After the creep heard she was dead, he was going to pick up where she left off."

Kim noticed the weapon wavering in Laura Ryan's hand and took a deep breath. "Was that why you took both Evelyn and Jameson's cell phones, because your phone number was on them?"

"I'm not talking to you anymore. Get moving!"

Kim spoke in a soft voice. "What's the hurry? We need to talk."

"No, we don't. There's nothing more to be said."

"I'm not leaving my apartment with you," Kim said.

"Then I'll shoot you here." Laura Ryan raised her gun and aimed it at Kim's chest.

The door opened quietly behind her, and Bert St. Croix said, "That wouldn't be smart."

Bert had her automatic drawn and ready.

Laura gasped and lowered her weapon. Bert snatched it away, handcuffed Laura and read her her rights.

"Backup is on the way, Kim," Bert said. "I thought we agreed it was a stupid idea to set yourself up as a target."

"It was," Kim agreed. "But I got to a point where I didn't have a better idea. There's a pair of earrings Evelyn was wearing when Laura murdered her. We saw Laura wearing them yesterday evening. I bet she still has them."

"I'll arrange for a search warrant."

"I wasn't planning to kill, Evelyn," Laura said. "She's the one who pulled out the gun. I told her what I thought of her and then I guess I might have threatened to kill her if she tried to ruin Thom's career. I was furious. She aimed the gun at me and waved it in my face. Well, I lost it. We fought for possession of the weapon and it just sort of went off."

"Did it sort of go off when you shot her in the back as well?" Bert asked.

"I don't remember doing that."

"Where's Evelyn's cell phone, Laura? What did you do with it?"

Laura looked away. "I might have disposed of it in a dumpster somewhere."

"And Richard Jameson?"

"The man contacted me. He knew. He intended to blackmail me too."

"He figured out you killed her, right? So I guess you decided you had to kill him as well?"

Laura Ryan didn't answer.

"And Kim?" Bert said.

"Another troublemaker. I'm not talking to you anymore. I want to call a lawyer."

"You have that right."

Bert turned the woman over to two uniformed patrolmen who arrived a few minutes later. When they were gone, she poked a finger at Kim. "I hope you realize how lucky you are that I have a lead foot on the gas. If I hadn't put on my emergency siren and lights, you'd probably be dead by now."

"I had a kitchen knife ready just in case."

Bert shook her head. "Librarians are a blood-thirsty lot."

"Some of us," Kim said.

All Kim could think about was that Mike would finally be released. And yes, it had been worth taking a big risk.

Chapter Fifty-Nine

The party wasn't in full swing because the guest of honor hadn't arrived yet. Kim glanced around. It was really just a small gathering: Chuck and Louise and their two boys as well as Mike's daughters, Bert, and herself.

Kim heard a car pull up the driveway. Jean rushed to the large picture window in the living room. "It's Daddy! He's back."

"This is so great," Evie said.

As a group, they went toward the front hall foyer to greet Mike.

He had lost weight. "No hugs now," he said putting up a hand to ward them off. "I need to take a shower first. I'm pretty ripe."

"Phew! You can say that again," Bert agreed.

There was nervous laughter. Mike excused himself and hurried upstairs. Fred Lincoln entered the house.

"Thanks for picking Mike up from the jail," Bert said.

"Goes with the territory," Fred replied.

"I think what you did for Mike goes beyond any client-lawyer relationship," Kim said.

Fred grinned. "I'd say only about two per cent of my clients are innocent. I don't mind going the extra mile for one who is."

"We all appreciate it," Kim said.

"Yeah, we do," Bert agreed. Her eyes lingered on his face.

Kim didn't miss the fact that Fred Lincoln took Bert's hand and held it.

Mike returned soon in clean clothes, his hair damp, slicked back, and smelling fresh. "I'll never again take for granted showering in safety," he said.

Louise handed him a glass of wine. Other glasses were passed around. Each child received a glass of grape juice. Chuck placed his arm around his brother.

"So do you want to offer a toast, Mike?"

"Sure." Mike thought for a moment, then raised his glass. "To the best family and friends a man could ever ask for." He looked around the room. "You saved my life. I feel humble and grateful." He took a swallow of his drink. "Yesterday is over. It's past history. Today is a gift."

"Is that why they call it the present?" Jean asked, her look innocent.

There were laughs and smiles.

"Good observation," Mike said, hugging his younger daughter. "Let's drink to tomorrow, to the future. To better days to come."

They all raised their glasses and drank.

"I love you all," he said. But he looked directly at Kim as he spoke. His eyes told her everything she needed to know.

Tears welled in Kim's eyes. She did her best to brush them away. Life was going to be better for them from here on. Her intuition told her so.

About the Author

Multiple award-winning author Jacqueline Seewald has taught creative, expository and technical writing at the university level as well as high school English. She also worked as an academic librarian and an educational media specialist. Fourteen of her books of fiction have been published. Her short stories, poems, essays, reviews and articles have appeared in hundreds of publications. She enjoys spending time with family and friends when she isn't writing. This is the fourth Kim Reynolds novel. Previous novels in this series are *The Inferno Collection, The Drowning Pool,* and *The Truth Sleuth*.